Full of gloom, the Pevensie children are waiting at the railway station for the train to take them back to school. Lucy feels a sudden tug, then Edmund does, and a minute later Peter and Susan do too. In a trice the station has vanished, and they find themselves in an overgrown wood near the sea, close by the ruins of their former castle, Cair Paravel. They are back in the magical land of Narnia where they had such wonderful times when they ruled as Kings and Queens (in *The Lion, the Witch and the Wardrobe*).

But something is very wrong. Their glorious castle lies in ruins and everywhere is strangely silent and empty. With the startling arrival of the Dwarf, they learn of the sad fate that has befallen Narnia. Civil war is now destroying the land as brave Prince Caspian, realising his uncle King Miraz's evil ways, is trying to regain the kingdom that is rightfully his. But Caspian needs help and, with the guidance of Aslan, the children take up the challenge to save Narnia and restore the long lost days of freedom and happiness.

THE CHRONICLES OF NARNIA
are all available from Collins

In reading order
The Magician's Nephew
The Lion, the Witch and the Wardrobe
The Horse and His Boy
Prince Caspian
The Voyage of the *Dawn Treader*
The Silver Chair
The Last Battle

C. S. LEWIS

Prince Caspian

The return to Narnia

illustrated by
Pauline Baynes

Grafton

This edition produced for The Book People Ltd,
Hall Wood Avenue, Haydock, St Helens WA11 9UL

First published in Great Britain by Geoffrey Bles 1951
First published by Collins in paperback 1980

Collins is an imprint of HarperCollins*Publishers* Ltd,
77-85 Fulham Palace Road, Hammersmith, London W6 8JB

ISBN 0 00 775500 7

Printed and bound in Great Britain by
Bookmarque Ltd, Croydon, Surrey

To Mary Clare Havard

CONTENTS

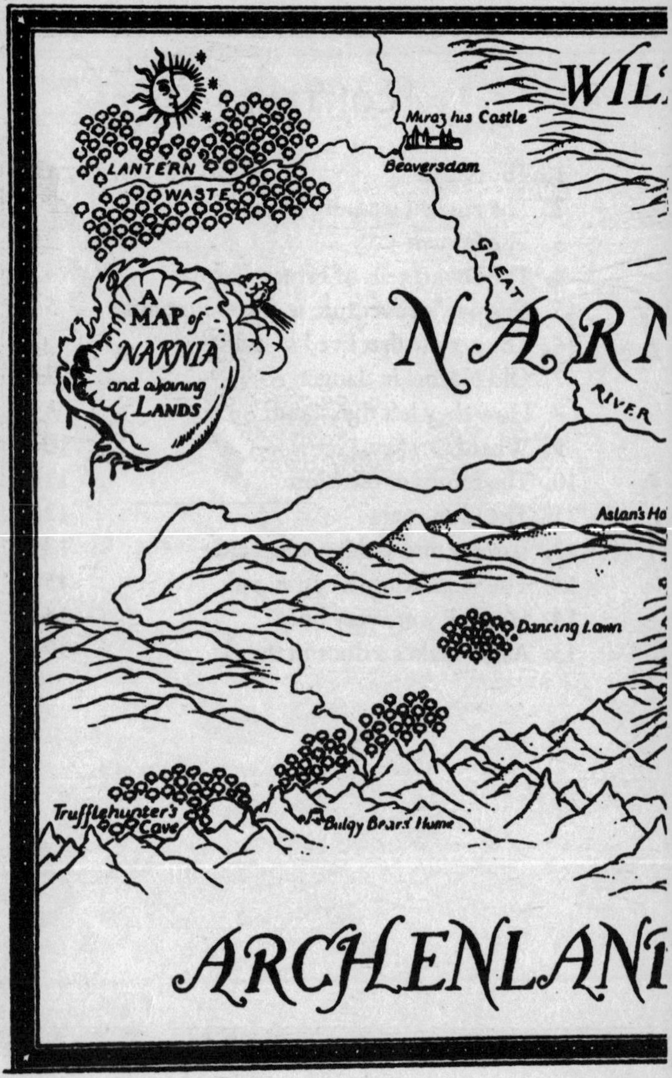

LANTERN
WASTE
A MAP of NARNIA and ajoining LANDS
Miraz his Castle
Beaversdam
GREAT
RIVER
Dancing Lawn
Trufflehunter's Cave
Bulgy Bears' Home

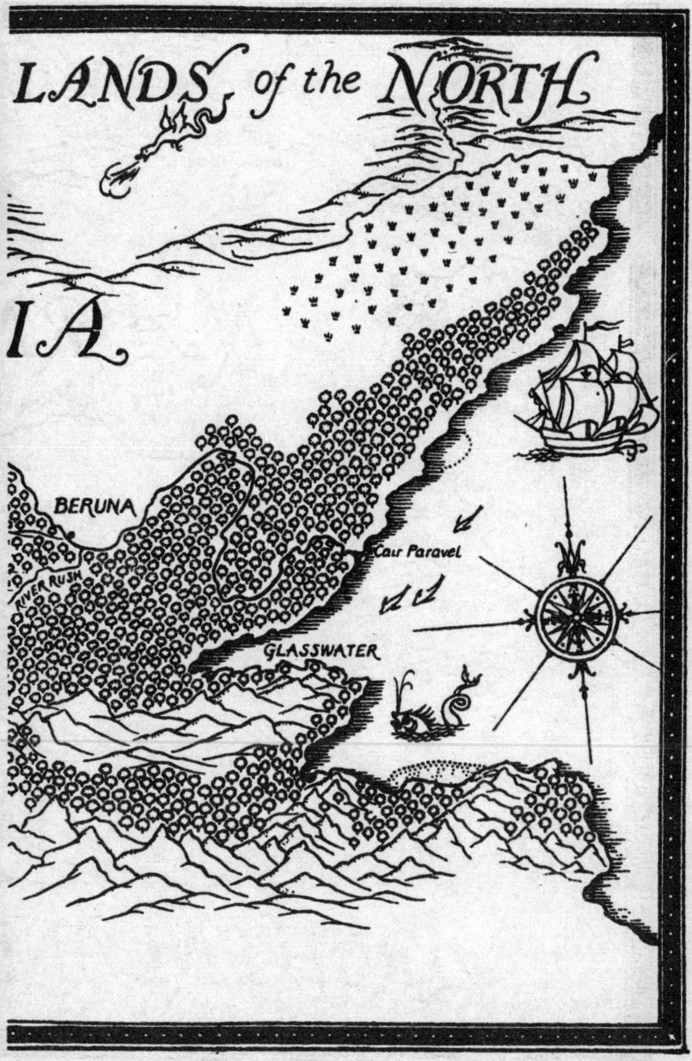
LANDS of the NORTH
IA
BERUNA
RIVER RUSH
Cair Paravel
GLASSWATER

CHAPTER ONE

THE ISLAND

ONCE there were four children whose names were Peter, Susan, Edmund, and Lucy, and it has been told in another book called *The Lion, the Witch and the Wardrobe* how they had a remarkable adventure. They had opened the door of a magic wardrobe and found themselves in a quite different world from ours, and in that different world they had become Kings and Queens in a country called Narnia. While they were in Narnia they seemed to reign for years and years; but when they came back through the door and found themselves in England again, it all seemed to have taken no time at all. At any rate, no one noticed that they had ever been away, and they never told anyone except one very wise grown-up.

That had all happened a year ago, and now all four of them were sitting on a seat at a railway station with trunks and playboxes piled up round them. They were, in fact, on their way back to school. They had travelled together as far as this station, which was a junction; and here, in a few minutes, one train would arrive and take the girls away to one school, and in about half an hour another train would arrive and the boys would go off to another school. The first part of the journey, when they were all together, always seemed to be part of the holidays; but now when they would be saying good-bye and going different ways so soon, everyone felt that the holidays were really over and everyone felt their term-time feelings beginning again, and they were all rather gloomy and no one could think of anything to say. Lucy was going to boarding school for the first time.

It was an empty, sleepy, country station and there was hardly anyone on the platform except themselves. Suddenly Lucy gave a sharp little cry, like someone who has been stung by a wasp.

"What's up, Lu?" said Edmund – and then suddenly broke off and made a noise like "Ow!"

"What on earth –" began Peter, and then he too suddenly changed what he had been going to say. Instead, he said, "Susan, let go! What are you doing? Where are you dragging me to?"

"I'm not touching you," said Susan. "Someone is pulling *me*. Oh – oh – oh – stop it!"

Everyone noticed that all the others' faces had gone very white.

"I felt just the same," said Edmund in a breathless voice. "As if I were being dragged along. A most frightful pulling – ugh! it's beginning again."

"Me too," said Lucy. "Oh, I can't bear it."

"Look sharp!" shouted Edmund. "All catch hands and keep together. This is magic – I can tell by the feeling. Quick!"

"Yes," said Susan. "Hold hands. Oh, I do wish it would stop – oh!"

Next moment the luggage, the seat, the platform, and the station had completely vanished. The four children, holding hands and panting, found themselves standing in a woody place – such a woody place that branches were sticking into them and there was hardly room to move. They all rubbed their eyes and took a deep breath.

"Oh, Peter!" exclaimed Lucy. "Do you think we can possibly have got back to Narnia?"

"It might be anywhere," said Peter. "I can't see a yard in

all these trees. Let's try to get into the open – if there is any open."

With some difficulty, and with some stings from nettles and pricks from thorns, they struggled out of the thicket. Then they had another surprise. Everything became much brighter, and after a few steps they found themselves at the edge of the wood, looking down on a sandy beach. A few yards away a very calm sea was falling on the sand with such tiny ripples that it made hardly any sound. There was no land in sight and no clouds in the sky. The sun was about where it ought to be at ten o'clock in the morning, and the sea was a dazzling blue. They stood sniffing in the sea-smell.

"By Jove!" said Peter. "This is good enough."

Five minutes later everyone was barefooted and wading in the cool clear water.

"This is better than being in a stuffy train on the way back to Latin and French and Algebra!" said Edmund. And then for quite a long time there was no more talking, only splashing and looking for shrimps and crabs.

"All the same," said Susan presently, "I suppose we'll have to make some plans. We shall want something to eat before long."

"We've got the sandwiches Mother gave us for the journey," said Edmund. "At least I've got mine."

"Not me," said Lucy. "Mine were in my little bag."

"So were mine," said Susan.

"Mine are in my coat-pocket, there on the beach," said Peter. "That'll be two lunches among four. This isn't going to be such fun."

"At present," said Lucy, "I want something to drink more than something to eat."

Everyone else now felt thirsty, as one usually is after wading in salt water under a hot sun.

"It's like being shipwrecked," remarked Edmund. "In the books they always find springs of clear, fresh water on the island. We'd better go and look for them."

"Does that mean we have to go back into all that thick wood?" said Susan.

"Not a bit of it," said Peter. "If there are streams they're bound to come down to the sea, and if we walk along the beach we're bound to come to them."

They all now waded back and went first across the smooth, wet sand and then up to the dry, crumbly sand that sticks to one's toes, and began putting on their shoes and socks. Edmund and Lucy wanted to leave them behind and do their exploring with bare feet, but Susan said this would be a mad thing to do. "We might never find them again," she pointed out, "and we shall want them if we're still here when night comes and it begins to be cold."

When they were dressed again they set out along the shore with the sea on their left hand and the wood on their right. Except for an occasional seagull it was a very quiet place. The wood was so thick and tangled that they could hardly see into it at all; and nothing in it moved – not a bird, not even an insect.

Shells and seaweed and anemones, or tiny crabs in rock-pools, are all very well, but you soon get tired of them if you are thirsty. The children's feet, after the change from the cool water, felt hot and heavy. Susan and Lucy had raincoats to carry. Edmund had put down his coat on the station seat just before the magic overtook them, and he and Peter took it in turns to carry Peter's great-coat.

Presently the shore began to curve round to the right.

About quarter of an hour later, after they had crossed a rocky ridge which ran out into a point, it made quite a sharp turn. Their backs were now to the part of the sea which had met them when they first came out of the wood, and now, looking ahead, they could see across the water another shore, thickly wooded like the one they were exploring.

"I wonder, is that an island or do we join on to it presently?" said Lucy.

"Don't know," said Peter and they all plodded on in silence.

The shore that they were walking on drew nearer and nearer to the opposite shore, and as they came round each promontory the children expected to find the place where the two joined. But in this they were disappointed. They came to some rocks which they had to climb and from the top they could see a fair way ahead and – "Oh bother!" said Edmund, "it's no good. We shan't be able to get to those other woods at all. We're on an island!"

It was true. At this point the channel between them and the opposite coast was only about thirty or forty yards wide; but they could now see that this was its narrowest place. After that, their own coast bent round to the right again and they could see open sea between it and the mainland. It was obvious that they had already come much more than half-way round the island.

"Look!" said Lucy suddenly. "What's that?" She pointed to a long, silvery, snake-like thing that lay across the beach.

"A stream! A stream!" shouted the others, and, tired as they were, they lost no time in clattering down the rocks and racing to the fresh water. They knew that the stream would be better to drink farther up, away from the beach, so they went at once to the spot where it came out of the wood. The trees were as thick as ever, but the stream had made itself a deep course between high mossy banks so that by stooping you could follow it up in a sort of tunnel of leaves. They dropped on their knees by the first brown, dimply pool and drank and drank, and dipped their faces in the water, and then dipped their arms in up to the elbow.

"Now," said Edmund, "what about those sandwiches?"

"Oh, hadn't we better save them?" said Susan. "We may need them far worse later on."

"I do wish," said Lucy, "now that we're not thirsty, we could go on feeling as not-hungry as we did when we *were* thirsty."

"But what about those sandwiches?" repeated Edmund. "There's no good saving them till they go bad. You've got to remember it's a good deal hotter here than in England and we've been carrying them about in pockets for hours." So they got out the two packets and divided them into four portions, and nobody had quite enough, but it was a great deal better than nothing. Then they talked about their plans for the next meal. Lucy wanted to go back to the sea and catch shrimps, until someone pointed out that they had no nets. Edmund said they must gather gulls' eggs from the rocks, but when they came to think of it they couldn't remember having seen any gulls' eggs and wouldn't be able to cook them if they found any. Peter thought to himself that unless they had some stroke of luck they would soon be glad to eat eggs raw, but he didn't see any point in saying this out loud. Susan said it was a pity they had eaten the sandwiches so soon. One or two tempers very nearly got lost at this stage. Finally Edmund said:

"Look here. There's only one thing to be done. We must explore the wood. Hermits and knights-errant and people like that always manage to live somehow if they're in a forest. They find roots and berries and things."

"What sort of roots?" asked Susan.

"I always thought it meant roots of trees," said Lucy.

"Come on," said Peter, "Ed is right. And we must try to do something. And it'll be better than going out into the glare and the sun again."

So they all got up and began to follow the stream. It was very hard work. They had to stoop under branches and climb over branches, and they blundered through great masses of stuff like rhododendrons and tore their clothes and got their feet wet in the stream; and still there was no noise at all except the noise of the stream and the noises they were making themselves. They were beginning to get very tired of it when they noticed a delicious smell, and then a flash of bright colour high above them at the top of the right bank.

"I say!" exclaimed Lucy. "I do believe that's an apple tree."

It was. They panted up the steep bank, forced their way through some brambles, and found themselves standing round an old tree that was heavy with large yellowish-golden apples as firm and juicy as you could wish to see.

"And this is not the only tree," said Edmund with his mouth full of apple. "Look there – and there."

"Why, there are dozens of them," said Susan, throwing away the core of her first apple and picking her second. "This must have been an orchard – long, long ago, before the place went wild and the wood grew up."

"Then this was once an inhabited island," said Peter.

"And what's that?" said Lucy, pointing ahead.

"By Jove, it's a wall," said Peter. "An old stone wall."

Pressing their way between the laden branches they reached the wall. It was very old, and broken down in places, with moss and wallflowers growing on it, but it was higher than all but the tallest trees. And when they came quite close to it they found a great arch which must once have had a gate in it but was now almost filled up with the largest of all the apple trees. They had to break some of the branches to get past, and when they had done so they all blinked because the daylight became suddenly much brighter. They found themselves in a wide open place with walls all round it. In here there were no trees, only level grass and daisies, and ivy, and grey walls. It was a bright, secret, quiet place, and rather sad; and all four stepped out into the middle of it, glad to be able to straighten their backs and move their limbs freely.

CHAPTER TWO

THE ANCIENT TREASURE HOUSE

"THIS wasn't a garden," said Susan presently. "It was a castle and this must have been the courtyard."

"I see what you mean," said Peter. "Yes. That is the remains of a tower. And there is what used to be a flight of steps going up to the top of the walls. And look at those other steps – the broad, shallow ones – going up to that doorway. It must have been the door into the great hall."

"Ages ago, by the look of it," said Edmund.

"Yes, ages ago," said Peter. "I wish we could find out who the people were that lived in this castle; and how long ago."

"It gives me a queer feeling," said Lucy.

"Does it, Lu?" said Peter, turning and looking hard at her. "Because it does the same to me. It is the queerest thing that has happened this queer day. I wonder where we are and what it all means?"

While they were talking they had crossed the courtyard and gone through the other doorway into what had once been the hall. This was now very like the courtyard, for the roof had long since disappeared and it was merely another space of grass and daisies, except that it was shorter and narrower and the walls were higher. Across the far end there was a kind of terrace about three feet higher than the rest.

"I wonder, was it really the hall?" said Susan. "What is that terrace kind of thing?"

"Why, you silly," said Peter (who had become strangely

excited), "don't you see? That was the dais where the High Table was, where the King and the great lords sat. Anyone would think you had forgotten that we ourselves were once Kings and Queens and sat on a dais just like that, in our great hall."

"In our castle of Cair Paravel," continued Susan in a dreamy and rather sing-song voice, "at the mouth of the great river of Narnia. How could I forget?"

"How it all comes back!" said Lucy. "We could pretend we were in Cair Paravel now. This hall must have been very like the great hall we feasted in."

"But unfortunately without the feast," said Edmund. "It's getting late, you know. Look how long the shadows are. And have you noticed that it isn't so hot?"

"We shall need a camp-fire if we've got to spend the night here," said Peter. "I've got matches. Let's go and see if we can collect some dry wood."

Everyone saw the sense of this, and for the next half-hour they were busy. The orchard through which they had first come into the ruins turned out not to be a good place for firewood. They tried the other side of the castle, passing out of the hall by a little side door into a maze of stony humps and hollows which must once have been passages and smaller rooms but was now all nettles and wild roses. Beyond this they found a wide gap in the castle wall and stepped through it into a wood of darker and bigger trees where they found dead branches and rotten wood and sticks and dry leaves and fir-cones in plenty. They went to and fro with bundles until they had a good pile on the dais. At the fifth journey they found the well, just outside the hall, hidden in weeds, but clean and fresh and deep when they had cleared these away.

The remains of a stone pavement ran half-way round it. Then the girls went out to pick some more apples and the boys built the fire, on the dais and fairly close to the corner between two walls, which they thought would be the snuggest and warmest place. They had great difficulty in lighting it and used a lot of matches, but they succeeded in the end. Finally, all four sat down with their backs to the wall and their faces to the fire. They tried roasting some of the apples on the ends of sticks. But roast apples are not much good without sugar, and they are too hot to eat with your fingers till they are too cold to be worth eating. So they had to content themselves with raw apples, which, as Edmund said, made one realize that school suppers weren't so bad after all – "I shouldn't mind a good thick slice of bread and margarine this minute," he added. But the spirit of adventure was rising in them all, and no one really wanted to be back at school.

Shortly after the last apple had been eaten, Susan went

out to the well to get another drink. When she came back she was carrying something in her hand.

"Look," she said in a rather choking kind of voice. "I found it by the well." She handed it to Peter and sat down. The others thought she looked and sounded as if she might be going to cry. Edmund and Lucy eagerly bent forward to see what was in Peter's hand – a little, bright thing that gleamed in the firelight.

"Well, I'm – I'm jiggered," said Peter, and his voice also sounded queer. Then he handed it to the others.

All now saw what it was – a little chess-knight, ordinary in size but extraordinarily heavy because it was made of pure gold; and the eyes in the horse's head were two tiny little rubies – or rather one was, for the other had been knocked out.

"Why!" said Lucy, "it's exactly like one of the golden chessmen we used to play with when we were Kings and Queens at Cair Paravel."

"Cheer up, Su," said Peter to his other sister.

"I can't help it," said Susan. "It brought back – oh, such lovely times. And I remembered playing chess with fauns and good giants, and the mer-people singing in the sea, and my beautiful horse – and – and –"

"Now," said Peter in a quite different voice, "it's about time we four started using our brains."

"What about?" asked Edmund.

"Have none of you guessed where we are?" said Peter.

"Go on, go on," said Lucy. "I've felt for hours that there was some wonderful mystery hanging over this place."

"Fire ahead, Peter," said Edmund. "We're all listening."

"We are in the ruins of Cair Paravel itself," said Peter.

"But, I say," replied Edmund. "I mean, how do you make that out? This place has been ruined for ages. Look at all those big trees growing right up to the gates. Look at the very stones. Anyone can see that nobody has lived here for hundreds of years."

"I know," said Peter. "That is the difficulty. But let's leave that out for the moment. I want to take the points one by one. First point: this hall is exactly the same shape and size as the hall at Cair Paravel. Just picture a roof on this, and a coloured pavement instead of grass, and tapestries on the walls, and you get our royal banqueting hall."

No one said anything.

"Second point," continued Peter. "The castle well is exactly where our well was, a little to the south of the great hall; and it is exactly the same size and shape."

Again there was no reply.

"Third point: Susan has just found one of our old chessmen – or something as like one of them as two peas."

Still nobody answered.

"Fourth point. Don't you remember – it was the very day before the ambassadors came from the King of Calormen – don't you remember planting the orchard outside the north gate of Cair Paravel? The greatest of all the wood-people, Pomona herself, came to put good spells on it. It was those very decent little chaps the moles who did the actual digging. Can you have forgotten that funny old Lilygloves, the chief mole, leaning on his spade and saying, 'Believe me, your Majesty, you'll be glad of these fruit trees one day.' And by Jove he was right."

"I do! I do!" said Lucy, and clapped her hands.

"But look here, Peter," said Edmund. "This must be all rot. To begin with, we didn't plant the orchard slap up against the gate. We wouldn't have been such fools."

"No, of course not," said Peter. "But it has grown up to the gate since."

"And for another thing," said Edmund, "Cair Paravel wasn't on an island."

"Yes, I've been wondering about that. But it was a what-do-you-call-it, a peninsula. Jolly nearly an island. Couldn't it have been made an island since our time? Somebody has dug a channel."

"But half a moment!" said Edmund. "You keep on saying *since our time*. But it's only a year ago since we came back from Narnia. And you want to make out that in one year castles have fallen down, and great forests have grown up, and little trees we saw planted ourselves have turned into a big old orchard, and goodness knows what else. It's all impossible."

"There's one thing," said Lucy. "If this is Cair Paravel there ought to be a door at this end of the dais. In fact we ought to be sitting with our backs against it at this moment. You know – the door that led down to the treasure chamber."

"I suppose there *isn't* a door," said Peter, getting up.

The wall behind them was a mass of ivy.

"We can soon find out," said Edmund, taking up one of the sticks that they had laid ready for putting on the fire. He began beating the ivied wall. Tap-tap went the stick against the stone; and again, tap-tap; and then, all at once, boom-boom, with a quite different sound, a hollow, wooden sound.

"Great Scott!" said Edmund.

"We must clear this ivy away," said Peter.

"Oh, do let's leave it alone," said Susan. "We can try it in the morning. If we've got to spend the night here I don't want an open door at my back and a great big black hole that anything might come out of, besides the draught and the damp. And it'll soon be dark."

"Susan! How can you?" said Lucy with a reproachful glance. But both the boys were too much excited to take any notice of Susan's advice. They worked at the ivy with their hands and with Peter's pocket-knife till the knife broke. After that they used Edmund's. Soon the whole place where they had been sitting was covered with ivy; and at last they had the door cleared.

"Locked, of course," said Peter.

"But the wood's all rotten," said Edmund. "We can pull it to bits in no time, and it will make extra firewood. Come on."

It took them longer than they expected and, before they had done, the great hall had grown dusky and the first star or two had come out overhead. Susan was not the only one who felt a slight shudder as the boys stood above the pile of splintered wood, rubbing the dirt off their hands and staring into the cold, dark opening they had made.

"Now for a torch," said Peter.

"Oh, what *is* the good?" said Susan. "And as Edmund said –"

"I'm not saying it now," Edmund interrupted. "I still don't understand, but we can settle that later. I suppose you're coming down, Peter?"

"We must," said Peter. "Cheer up, Susan. It's no good behaving like kids now that we are back in Narnia.

You're a Queen here. And anyway no one could go to sleep with a mystery like this on their minds."

They tried to use long sticks as torches but this was not a success. If you held them with the lighted end up they went out, and if you held them the other way they scorched your hand and the smoke got in your eyes. In the end they had to use Edmund's electric torch; luckily it had been a birthday present less than a week ago and the battery was almost new. He went first, with the light. Then came Lucy, then Susan, and Peter brought up the rear.

"I've come to the top of the steps," said Edmund.

"Count them," said Peter.

"One – two – three," said Edmund, as he went cautiously down, and so up to sixteen. "And this is the bottom," he shouted back.

"Then it really must be Cair Paravel," said Lucy. "There were sixteen." Nothing more was said till all four were standing in a knot together at the foot of the stairway. Then Edmund flashed his torch slowly round.

"O – o – o – oh!!" said all the children at once.

For now all knew that it was indeed the ancient treasure chamber of Cair Paravel where they had once reigned as Kings and Queens of Narnia. There was a kind of path up the middle (as it might be in a greenhouse), and along each side at intervals stood rich suits of armour, like knights guarding the treasures. In between the suits of armour, and on each side of the path, were shelves covered with precious things – necklaces and arm rings and finger rings and golden bowls and dishes and long tusks of ivory, brooches and coronets and chains of gold, and heaps of unset stones lying piled anyhow as if they were marbles or potatoes – diamonds, rubies, carbuncles, emeralds, topazes, and amethysts. Under the shelves stood great chests of oak strengthened with iron bars and heavily padlocked. And it was bitterly cold, and so still that they could hear themselves breathing, and the treasures were so covered with dust that unless they had realized where they were and remembered most of the things, they would hardly have known they were treasures. There was something sad and a little frightening about the place, because it all seemed so forsaken and long ago. That was why nobody said anything for at least a minute.

Then, of course, they began walking about and picking things up to look at. It was like meeting very old friends. If you had been there you would have heard them saying things like, "Oh look! Our coronation rings – do you remember first wearing this? – Why, this is the little brooch we all thought was lost – I say, isn't that the armour you wore in the great tournament in the Lone Islands? – do you remember the dwarf making that for me? – do you remember drinking out of that horn? – do you remember, do you remember?"

But suddenly Edmund said, "Look here. We mustn't waste the battery: goodness knows how often we shall need it. Hadn't we better take what we want and get out again?"

"We must take the gifts," said Peter. For long ago at a Christmas in Narnia he and Susan and Lucy had been given certain presents which they valued more than their whole kingdom. Edmund had had no gift, because he was not with them at the time. (This was his own fault, and you can read about it in the other book.)

They all agreed with Peter and walked up the path to the wall at the far end of the treasure chamber, and there, sure enough, the gifts were still hanging. Lucy's was the smallest for it was only a little bottle. But the bottle was made of diamond instead of glass, and it was still more than half full of the magical cordial which would heal almost every wound and every illness. Lucy said nothing and looked very solemn as she took her gift down from its place and slung the belt over her shoulder and once more felt the bottle at her side where it used to hang in the old days. Susan's gift had been a bow and arrows and a horn. The bow was still there, and the ivory quiver, full of well-feathered arrows, but – "Oh, Susan," said Lucy. "Where's the horn?"

"Oh bother, bother, bother," said Susan after she had thought for a moment. "I remember now. I took it with me the last day of all, the day we went hunting the White Stag. It must have got lost when we blundered back into that other place – England, I mean."

Edmund whistled. It was indeed a shattering loss; for this was an enchanted horn and, whenever you blew it, help was certain to come to you, wherever you were.

"Just the sort of thing that might come in handy in a place like this," said Edmund.

"Never mind," said Susan, "I've still got the bow." And she took it.

"Won't the string be perished, Su?" said Peter.

But whether by some magic in the air of the treasure chamber or not, the bow was still in working order. Archery and swimming were the things Susan was good at. In a moment she had bent the bow and then she gave one little pluck to the string. It twanged: a chirruping twang that vibrated through the whole room. And that one small noise brought back the old days to the children's minds more than anything that had happened yet. All the battles and hunts and feasts came rushing into their heads together.

Then she unstrung the bow again and slung the quiver at her side.

Next, Peter took down his gift – the shield with the great red lion on it, and the royal sword. He blew, and rapped them on the floor, to get off the dust. He fitted the shield on his arm and slung the sword by his side. He was afraid at first that it might be rusty and stick to the sheath. But it was not so. With one swift motion he drew it and held it up, shining in the torchlight.

"It is my sword Rhindon," he said; "with it I killed the Wolf." There was a new tone in his voice, and the others

all felt that he was really Peter the High King again. Then, after a little pause, everyone remembered that they must save the battery.

They climbed the stair again and made up a good fire and lay down close together for warmth. The ground was very hard and uncomfortable, but they fell asleep in the end.

CHAPTER THREE

THE DWARF

THE worst of sleeping out of doors is that you wake up so dreadfully early. And when you wake you have to get up because the ground is so hard that you are uncomfortable. And it makes matters worse if there is nothing but apples for breakfast and you have had nothing but apples for supper the night before. When Lucy had said – truly enough – that it was a glorious morning, there did not seem to be anything else nice to be said. Edmund said what everyone was feeling, "We've simply got to get off this island."

When they had drunk from the well and splashed their faces they all went down the stream again to the shore and stared at the channel which divided them from the mainland.

"We'll have to swim," said Edmund.

"It would be all right for Su," said Peter (Susan had won prizes for swimming at school). "But I don't know about the rest of us." By "the rest of us" he really meant Edmund who couldn't yet do two lengths at the school baths, and Lucy, who could hardly swim at all.

"Anyway," said Susan, "there may be currents. Father says it's never wise to bathe in a place you don't know."

"But, Peter," said Lucy, "look here. I know I can't swim for nuts at home – in England, I mean. But couldn't we all swim long ago – if it was long ago – when we were Kings and Queens in Narnia? We could ride then too, and do all sorts of things. Don't you think –?"

"Ah, but we were sort of grown-up then," said Peter.

"We reigned for years and years and learned to do things. Aren't we just back at our proper ages again now?"

"Oh!" said Edmund in a voice which made everyone stop talking and listen to him.

"I've just seen it all," he said.

"Seen what?" asked Peter.

"Why, the whole thing," said Edmund. "You know what we were puzzling about last night, that it was only a year ago since we left Narnia but everything looks as if no one had lived in Cair Paravel for hundreds of years? Well, don't you see? You know that, however long we seemed to have lived in Narnia, when we got back through the wardrobe it seemed to have taken no time at all?"

"Go on," said Susan. "I think I'm beginning to understand."

"And that means," continued Edmund, "that, once you're out of Narnia, you have no idea how Narnian time is going. Why shouldn't hundreds of years have gone past in Narnia while only one year has passed for us in England?"

"By Jove, Ed," said Peter. "I believe you've got it. In that sense it really was hundreds of years ago that we lived in Cair Paravel. And now we're coming back to Narnia just as if we were Crusaders or Anglo-Saxons or Ancient Britons or someone coming back to modern England?"

"How excited they'll be to see us –" began Lucy, but at the same moment everyone else said, "Hush!" or "Look!" For now something was happening.

There was a wooded point on the mainland a little to their right, and they all felt sure that just beyond that point must be the mouth of the river. And now, round that point there came into sight a boat. When it had cleared the point, it turned and began coming along the channel towards them. There were two people on board, one rowing, the other sitting in the stern and holding a bundle that twitched and moved as if it were alive. Both these people seemed to be soldiers. They had steel caps on their heads and light shirts of chain-mail. Their faces were bearded and hard. The children drew back from the beach into the wood and watched without moving a finger.

"This'll do," said the soldier in the stern when the boat had come about opposite to them.

"What about tying a stone to his feet, Corporal?" said the other, resting on his oars.

"Garn!" growled the other. "We don't need that, and we haven't brought one. He'll drown sure enough without a stone, as long as we've tied the cords right." With these words he rose and lifted his bundle. Peter now saw that it was really alive and was in fact a Dwarf, bound hand and foot but struggling as hard as he could. Next moment he heard a twang just beside his ear, and all at once the soldier threw up his arms, dropping the Dwarf into the bottom of the boat, and fell over into the water. He floundered away to the far bank and Peter knew that Susan's arrow had struck on his helmet. He turned and saw that she was very pale but was already fitting a second arrow to the string. But it was never used. As soon as he saw his companion fall, the other soldier, with a loud cry, jumped out of the boat on the far side, and he also floundered through the water (which was apparently just in his depth) and disappeared into the woods of the mainland.

"Quick! Before she drifts!" shouted Peter. He and Susan, fully dressed as they were, plunged in, and before the water was up to their shoulders their hands were on the side of the boat. In a few seconds they had hauled her to the bank and lifted the Dwarf out, and Edmund was busily engaged in cutting his bonds with the pocket knife. (Peter's sword would have been sharper, but a sword is very inconvenient for this sort of work because you can't hold it anywhere lower than the hilt.) When at last the Dwarf was free, he sat up, rubbed his arms and legs, and exclaimed:

"Well, whatever they say, you don't *feel* like ghosts."

Like most Dwarfs he was very stocky and deep-chested. He would have been about three feet high if he had been standing up, and an immense beard and whiskers of coarse red hair left little of his face to be seen except a beak-like nose and twinkling black eyes.

"Anyway," he continued, "ghosts or not, you've saved my life and I'm extremely obliged to you."

"But why should we be ghosts?" asked Lucy.

"I've been told all my life," said the Dwarf, "that these woods along the shore were as full of ghosts as they were of trees. That's what the story is. And that's why, when they want to get rid of anyone, they usually bring him down here (like they were doing with me) and say they'll leave him to the ghosts. But I always wondered if they didn't really drown 'em or cut their throats. I never quite believed in the ghosts. But those two cowards you've just shot believed all right. They were more frightened of taking me to my death than I was of going!"

"Oh," said Susan. "So that's why they both ran away."

"Eh? What's that?" said the Dwarf.

"They got away," said Edmund. "To the mainland."

"I wasn't shooting to kill, you know," said Susan. She would not have liked anyone to think she could miss at such a short range.

"Hm," said the Dwarf. "That's not so good. That may mean trouble later on. Unless they hold their tongues for their own sake."

"What were they going to drown you for?" asked Peter.

"Oh, I'm a dangerous criminal, I am," said the Dwarf cheerfully. "But that's a long story. Meantime, I was wondering if perhaps you were going to ask me to breakfast? You've no idea what an appetite it gives one, being executed."

"There's only apples," said Lucy dolefully.

"Better than nothing, but not so good as fresh fish," said the Dwarf. "It looks as if I'll have to ask you to breakfast instead. I saw some fishing tackle in that boat. And anyway, we must take her round to the other side of the

island. We don't want anyone from the mainland coming down and seeing her."

"I ought to have thought of that myself," said Peter.

The four children and the Dwarf went down to the water's edge, pushed off the boat with some difficulty, and scrambled aboard. The Dwarf at once took charge. The oars were of course too big for him to use, so Peter rowed and the Dwarf steered them north along the channel and presently eastward round the tip of the island. From here the children could see right up the river, and all the bays and headlands of the coast beyond it. They thought they could recognize bits of it, but the woods, which had grown up since their time, made everything look very different.

When they had come round into open sea on the east of the island, the Dwarf took to fishing. They had an excellent catch of pavenders, a beautiful rainbow-coloured fish which they all remembered eating in Cair Paravel in the old days. When they had caught enough they ran the boat up into a little creek and moored her to a tree. The Dwarf, who was a most capable person (and, indeed, though one meets bad Dwarfs, I never heard of a Dwarf who was a fool), cut the fish open, cleaned them, and said:

"Now, what we want next is some firewood."

"We've got some up at the castle," said Edmund.

The Dwarf gave a low whistle. "Beards and bedsteads!" he said. "So there really is a castle, after all?"

"It's only a ruin," said Lucy.

The Dwarf stared round at all four of them with a very curious expression on his face. "And who on earth – ?" he began, but then broke off and said, "No matter. Breakfast first. But one thing before we go on. Can you lay your hand on your hearts and tell me I'm really alive? Are you sure I wasn't drowned and we're not all ghosts together?"

When they had all reassured him, the next question was how to carry the fish. They had nothing to string them on and no basket. They had to use Edmund's hat in the end because no one else had a hat. He would have made much more fuss about this if he had not by now been so ravenously hungry.

At first the Dwarf did not seem very comfortable in the

castle. He kept looking round and sniffing and saying, "H'm. Looks a bit spooky after all. Smells like ghosts, too." But he cheered up when it came to lighting the fire and showing them how to roast the fresh pavenders in the embers. Eating hot fish with no forks, and one pocket knife between five people, is a messy business and there were several burnt fingers before the meal was ended; but, as it was now nine o'clock and they had been up since five, nobody minded the burns so much as you might have expected. When everyone had finished off with a drink from the well and an apple or so, the Dwarf produced a pipe about the size of his own arm, filled it, lit it, blew a great cloud of fragrant smoke, and said, "Now."

"You tell us your story first," said Peter. "And then we'll tell you ours."

"Well," said the Dwarf, "as you've saved my life it is only fair you should have your own way. But I hardly know where to begin. First of all I'm a messenger of King Caspian's."

"Who's he?" asked four voices all at once.

"Caspian the Tenth, King of Narnia, and long may he reign!" answered the Dwarf. "That is to say, he ought to be King of Narnia and we hope he will be. At present he is only King of us Old Narnians – "

"What do you mean by *old* Narnians, please?" asked Lucy.

"Why, that's us," said the Dwarf. "We're a kind of rebellion, I suppose."

"I see," said Peter. "And Caspian is the chief Old Narnian."

"Well, in a manner of speaking," said the Dwarf,

scratching his head. "But he's really a New Narnian himself, a Telmarine, if you follow me."

"I don't," said Edmund.

"It's worse than the Wars of the Roses," said Lucy.

"Oh dear," said the Dwarf. "I'm doing this very badly. Look here: I think I'll have to go right back to the beginning and tell you how Caspian grew up in his uncle's court and how he comes to be on our side at all. But it'll be a long story."

"All the better," said Lucy. "We love stories."

So the Dwarf settled down and told his tale. I shall not give it to you in his words, putting in all the children's questions and interruptions, because it would take too long and be confusing, and, even so, it would leave out some points that the children only heard later. But the gist of the story, as they knew it in the end, was as follows.

CHAPTER FOUR

THE DWARF TELLS OF PRINCE CASPIAN

PRINCE CASPIAN lived in a great castle in the centre of Narnia with his uncle, Miraz, the King of Narnia, and his aunt, who had red hair and was called Queen Prunaprismia. His father and mother were dead and the person whom Caspian loved best was his nurse, and though (being a prince) he had wonderful toys which would do almost anything but talk, he liked best the last hour of the day when the toys had all been put back in their cupboards and Nurse would tell him stories.

He did not care much for his uncle and aunt, but about twice a week his uncle would send for him and they would walk up and down together for half an hour on the terrace at the south side of the castle. One day, while they were doing this, the King said to him,

"Well, boy, we must soon teach you to ride and use a sword. You know that your aunt and I have no children, so it looks as if you might have to be King when I'm gone. How shall you like that, eh?"

"I don't know, Uncle," said Caspian.

"Don't know, eh?" said Miraz. "Why, I should like to know what more anyone could wish for!"

"All the same, I *do* wish," said Caspian.

"What do you wish?" asked the King.

"I wish – I wish – I wish I could have lived in the Old Days," said Caspian. (He was only a very little boy at the time.)

Up till now King Miraz had been talking in the tiresome way that some grown-ups have, which makes it quite clear that they are not really interested in what you are saying, but now he suddenly gave Caspian a very sharp look.

"Eh? What's that?" he said. "What old days do you mean?"

"Oh, don't you know, Uncle?" said Caspian. "When everything was quite different. When all the animals could talk, and there were nice people who lived in the streams and the trees. Naiads and Dryads they were called. And there were Dwarfs. And there were lovely little Fauns in all the woods. They had feet like goats. And –"

"That's all nonsense, for babies," said the King sternly. "Only fit for babies, do you hear? You're getting too old for that sort of stuff. At your age you ought to be thinking of battles and adventures, not fairy tales."

"Oh, but there *were* battles and adventures in those days," said Caspian. "Wonderful adventures. Once there was a White Witch and she made herself Queen of the whole country. And she made it so that it was always winter. And then two boys and two girls came from somewhere and so they killed the Witch and they were made Kings and Queens of Narnia, and their names were Peter and Susan and Edmund and Lucy. And so they reigned for ever so long and everyone had a lovely time, and it was all because of Aslan –"

"Who's he?" said Miraz. And if Caspian had been a very little older, the tone of his uncle's voice would have warned him that it would be wiser to shut up. But he babbled on,

"Oh, don't you know?" he said. "Aslan is the great Lion who comes from over the sea."

"Who has been telling you all this nonsense?" said the King in a voice of thunder. Caspian was frightened and said nothing.

"Your Royal Highness," said King Miraz, letting go of Caspian's hand, which he had been holding till now, "I insist upon being answered. Look me in the face. Who has been telling you this pack of lies?"

"N – Nurse," faltered Caspian, and burst into tears.

"Stop that noise," said his uncle, taking Caspian by the shoulders and giving him a shake. "Stop it. And never let me catch you talking – or *thinking* either – about all those silly stories again. There never were those Kings and Queens. How could there be two Kings at the same time? And there's no such person as Aslan. And there are no such things as lions. And there never was a time when animals could talk. Do you hear?"

"Yes, Uncle," sobbed Caspian.

"Then let's have no more of it," said the King. Then he called to one of the gentlemen-in-waiting who were standing at the far end of the terrace and said in a cold voice, "Conduct His Royal Highness to his apartments and send His Royal Highness's nurse to me AT ONCE."

Next day Caspian found what a terrible thing he had done, for Nurse had been sent away without even being allowed to say good-bye to him, and he was told he was to have a Tutor.

Caspian missed his nurse very much and shed many tears; and because he was so miserable, he thought about the old stories of Narnia far more than before. He dreamed of Dwarfs and Dryads every night and tried very hard to make the dogs and cats in the castle talk to him. But the dogs only wagged their tails and the cats only purred.

Caspian felt sure that he would hate the new Tutor, but when the new Tutor arrived about a week later he turned

out to be the sort of person it is almost impossible not to like. He was the smallest, and also the fattest, man Caspian had ever seen. He had a long, silvery, pointed beard which came down to his waist, and his face, which was brown and covered with wrinkles, looked very wise, very ugly, and very kind. His voice was grave and his eyes were merry so that, until you got to know him really well, it was hard to know when he was joking and when he was serious. His name was Doctor Cornelius.

Of all his lessons with Doctor Cornelius the one that Caspian liked best was History. Up till now, except for Nurse's stories, he had known nothing about the History of Narnia, and he was very surprised to learn that the royal family were newcomers in the country.

"It was your Highness's ancestor, Caspian the First," said Doctor Cornelius, "who first conquered Narnia and made it his kingdom. It was he who brought all your nation into the country. You are not native Narnians at all. You are all Telmarines – that is, you all came from the Land of Telmar, far beyond the Western Mountains. That is why Caspian the First is called Caspian the Conqueror."

"Please, Doctor," asked Caspian one day, "who lived in Narnia before we all came here out of Telmar?"

"No men – or very few – lived in Narnia before the Telmarines took it," said Doctor Cornelius.

"Then who did my great-great-grandcesters conquer?"

"*Whom*, not *who*, your Highness," said Doctor Cornelius. "Perhaps it is time to turn from History to Grammar."

"Oh please, not yet," said Caspian. "I mean, wasn't

there a battle? Why is he called Caspian the Conqueror if there was nobody to fight with him?"

"I said there were very few *men* in Narnia," said the Doctor, looking at the little boy very strangely through his great spectacles.

For a moment Caspian was puzzled and then suddenly his heart gave a leap. "Do you mean," he gasped, "that there were other things? Do you mean it was like in the stories? Were there –?"

"Hush!" said Doctor Cornelius, laying his head very close to Caspian's. "Not a word more. Don't you know your Nurse was sent away for telling you about Old Narnia? The King doesn't like it. If he found me telling you secrets, you'd be whipped and I should have my head cut off."

"But why?" asked Caspian.

"It is high time we turned to Grammar now," said Doctor Cornelius in a loud voice. "Will your Royal Highness be pleased to open Pulverulentus Siccus at the fourth page of his *Grammatical garden or the Arbour of Accidence pleasantlie open'd to Tender Wits?*"

After that it was all nouns and verbs till lunchtime, but I don't think Caspian learned much. He was too excited. He felt sure that Doctor Cornelius would not have said so much unless he meant to tell him more sooner or later.

In this he was not disappointed. A few days later his Tutor said, "Tonight I am going to give you a lesson in Astronomy. At dead of night two noble planets, Tarva and Alambil, will pass within one degree of each other. Such a conjunction has not occurred for two hundred years, and your Highness will not live to see it again. It will be best if you go to bed a little earlier than usual. When the time of the conjunction draws near I will come and wake you."

This didn't seem to have anything to do with Old Narnia, which was what Caspian really wanted to hear about, but getting up in the middle of the night is always interesting and he was moderately pleased. When he went to bed that night, he thought at first that he would not be able to sleep; but he soon dropped off and it seemed only a few minutes before he felt someone gently shaking him.

He sat up in bed and saw that the room was full of moonlight. Doctor Cornelius, muffled in a hooded robe and holding a small lamp in his hand, stood by the bedside.

Caspian remembered at once what they were going to do. He got up and put on some clothes. Athough it was a summer night he felt colder than he had expected and was quite glad when the Doctor wrapped him in a robe like his own and gave him a pair of warm, soft buskins for his feet. A moment later, both muffled so that they could hardly be seen in the dark corridors, and both shod so that they made almost no noise, master and pupil left the room.

Caspian followed the Doctor through many passages and up several staircases, and at last, through a little door in a turret, they came out upon the leads. On one side were the battlements, on the other a steep roof; below them, all shadowy and shimmery, the castle gardens; above them, stars and moon. Presently they came to another door, which led into the great central tower of the whole castle: Doctor Cornelius unlocked it and they began to climb the dark winding stair of the tower. Caspian was becoming excited; he had never been allowed up this stair before.

It was long and steep, but when they came out on the roof of the tower and Caspian had got his breath, he felt that it had been well worth it. Away on his right he could see, rather indistinctly, the Western Mountains. On his left was the gleam of the Great River, and everything was so quiet that he could hear the sound of the waterfall at Beaversdam, a mile away. There was no difficulty in picking out the two stars they had come to see. They hung rather low in the southern sky, almost as bright as two little moons and very close together.

"Are they going to have a collision?" he asked in an awe-struck voice.

"Nay, dear Prince," said the Doctor (and he too spoke in a whisper). "The great lords of the upper sky know the steps of their dance too well for that. Look well upon them. Their meeting is fortunate and means some great good for the sad realm of Narnia. Tarva, the Lord of Victory, salutes Alambil, the Lady of Peace. They are just coming to their nearest."

"It's a pity that tree gets in the way," said Caspian. "We'd really see better from the West Tower, though it is not so high."

Doctor Cornelius said nothing for about two minutes, but stood still with his eyes fixed on Tarva and Alambil. Then he drew a deep breath and turned to Caspian.

"There," he said. "You have seen what no man now alive has seen, nor will see again. And you are right. We should have seen it even better from the smaller tower. I brought you here for another reason."

Caspian looked up at him, but the Doctor's hood concealed most of his face.

"The virtue of this tower," said Doctor Cornelius, "is that we have six empty rooms beneath us, and a long stair, and the door at the bottom of the stair is locked. We cannot be overheard."

"Are you going to tell me what you wouldn't tell me the other day?" said Caspian.

"I am," said the Doctor. "But remember. You and I must never talk about these things except here – on the very top of the Great Tower."

"No. That's a promise," said Caspian. "But do go on, please."

"Listen," said the Doctor. "All you have heard about Old Narnia is true. It is not the land of Men. It is the country of Aslan, the country of the Waking Trees and Visible Naiads, of Fauns and Satyrs, of Dwarfs and Giants, of the gods and the Centaurs, of Talking Beasts. It was against these that the first Caspian fought. It is you Telmarines who silenced the beasts and the trees and the fountains, and who killed and drove away the Dwarfs and Fauns, and are now trying to cover up even the memory of them. The King does not allow them to be spoken of."

"Oh, I do wish we hadn't," said Caspian. "And I *am* glad it was all true, even if it is all over."

"Many of your race wish that in secret," said Doctor Cornelius.

"But, Doctor," said Caspian, "why do you say *my* race? After all, I suppose you're a Telmarine too."

"Am I?" said the Doctor.

"Well, you're a Man anyway," said Caspian.

"Am I?" repeated the Doctor in a deeper voice, at the same moment throwing back his hood so that Caspian could see his face clearly in the moonlight.

All at once Caspian realized the truth and felt that he ought to have realized it long before. Doctor Cornelius was so small, and so fat, and had such a very long beard. Two thoughts came into his head at the same moment. One was a thought of terror – "He's not a real man, not a man at all, he's a *Dwarf*, and he's brought me up here to kill me." The other was sheer delight – "There are real Dwarfs still, and I've seen one at last."

"So you've guessed it in the end," said Doctor Cornelius. "Or guessed it nearly right. I'm not a pure Dwarf. I have human blood in me too. Many Dwarfs escaped in the great battles and lived on, shaving their beards and wearing high-heeled shoes and pretending to be men. They have mixed with your Telmarines. I am one of those, only a half-Dwarf, and if any of my kindred, the true Dwarfs, are still alive anywhere in the world, doubtless they would despise me and call me a traitor. But never in all these years have we forgotten our own people and all the other happy creatures of Narnia, and the long-lost days of freedom."

"I'm – I'm sorry, Doctor," said Caspian. "It wasn't my fault, you know."

"I am not saying these things in blame of you, dear Prince," answered the Doctor. "You may well ask why I say them at all. But I have two reasons. Firstly, because my old heart has carried these secret memories so long that it aches with them and would burst if I did not whisper them to you. But secondly, for this: that when you become King you may help us, for I know that you also, Telmarine though you are, love the Old Things."

"I do, I do," said Caspian. "But how can I help?"

"You can be kind to the poor remnants of the Dwarf people, like myself. You can gather learned magicians and try to find a way of awaking the trees once more. You can search through all the nooks and wild places of the land to see if any Fauns or Talking Beasts or Dwarfs are perhaps still alive in hiding."

"Do you think there are any?" asked Caspian eagerly.

"I don't know – I don't know," said the Doctor with a deep sigh. "Sometimes I am afraid there can't be. I have been looking for traces of them all my life. Sometimes I have thought I heard a Dwarf-drum in the mountains. Sometimes at night, in the woods, I thought I had caught a glimpse of Fauns and Satyrs dancing a long way off; but when I came to the place, there was never anything there. I have often despaired; but something always happens to start me hoping again. I don't know. But at least you can try to be a King like the High King Peter of old, and not like your uncle."

"Then it's true about the Kings and Queens too, and about the White Witch?" said Caspian.

"Certainly it is true," said Cornelius. "Their reign was the Golden Age in Narnia and the land has never forgotten them."

"Did they live in this castle, Doctor?"

"Nay, my dear," said the old man. "This castle is a thing of yesterday. Your great-great-grandfather built it. But when the two sons of Adam and the two daughters of Eve were made Kings and Queens of Narnia by Aslan himself, they lived in the castle of Cair Paravel. No man alive has seen that blessed place and perhaps even the ruins of it have now vanished. But we believe it was far from here, down at the mouth of the Great River, on the very shore of the sea."

"Ugh!" said Caspian with a shudder. "Do you mean in

the Black Woods? Where all the – the – you know, the ghosts live?"

"Your Highness speaks as you have been taught," said the Doctor. "But it is all lies. There are no ghosts there. That is a story invented by the Telmarines. Your Kings are in deadly fear of the sea because they can never quite forget that in all stories Aslan comes from over the sea. They don't want to go near it and they don't want anyone else to go near it. So they have let great woods grow up to cut their people off from the coast. But because they have quarrelled with the trees they are afraid of the woods. And because they are afraid of the woods they imagine that they are full of ghosts. And the Kings and great men, hating both the sea and the wood, partly believe these stories, and partly encourage them. They feel safer if no one in Narnia dares to go down to the coast and look out to sea – towards Aslan's land and the morning and the eastern end of the world."

There was a deep silence between them for a few minutes. Then Doctor Cornelius said, "Come. We have been here long enough. It is time to go down and to bed."

"Must we?" said Caspian. "I'd like to go on talking about these things for hours and hours and hours."

"Someone might begin looking for us, if we did that," said Doctor Cornelius.

CHAPTER FIVE

CASPIAN'S ADVENTURE IN THE MOUNTAINS

AFTER this, Caspian and his Tutor had many more secret conversations on the top of the Great Tower, and at each conversation Caspian learned more about Old Narnia, so that thinking and dreaming about the old days, and longing that they might come back, filled nearly all his spare hours. But of course he had not many hours to spare, for now his education was beginning in earnest. He learned sword-fighting and riding, swimming and diving, how to shoot with the bow and play on the recorder and the theorbo, how to hunt the stag and cut him up when he was dead, besides Cosmography, Rhetoric, Heraldry, Versification, and of course History, with a little Law, Physic, Alchemy, and Astronomy. Of Magic he learned only the theory, for Doctor Cornelius said the practical part was not proper study for princes. "And I myself," he added, "am only a very imperfect magician and can do only the smallest experiments." Of Navigation ("Which is a noble and heroical art," said the Doctor) he was taught nothing, because King Miraz disapproved of ships and the sea.

He also learned a great deal by using his own eyes and ears. As a little boy he had often wondered why he disliked his aunt, Queen Prunaprismia; he now saw that it was because she disliked him. He also began to see that Narnia was an unhappy country. The taxes were high and the laws were stern and Miraz was a cruel man.

After some years there came a time when the Queen seemed to be ill and there was a great deal of bustle and pother about her in the castle and doctors came and the courtiers whispered. This was in early summertime. And one night, while all this fuss was going on, Caspian was unexpectedly wakened by Doctor Cornelius after he had been only a few hours in bed.

"Are we going to do a little Astronomy, Doctor?" said Caspian.

"Hush!" said the Doctor. "Trust me and do exactly as I tell you. Put on all your clothes; you have a long journey before you."

Caspian was very surprised, but he had learned to have confidence in his Tutor and he began doing what he was told at once. When he was dressed the Doctor said, "I have a wallet for you. We must go into the next room and fill it with victuals from your Highness's supper table."

"My gentlemen-in-waiting will be there," said Caspian.

"They are fast asleep and will not wake," said the Doctor. "I am a very minor magician but I *can* at least contrive a charmed sleep."

They went into the antechamber and there, sure enough, the two gentlemen-in-waiting were, sprawling on chairs and snoring hard. Doctor Cornelius quickly cut up the remains of a cold chicken and some slices of venison and put them, with bread and an apple or so and a little flask of good wine, into the wallet which he then gave to Caspian. It fitted on by a strap over Caspian's shoulder, like a satchel you would use for taking books to school.

"Have you your sword?" asked the Doctor.

"Yes," said Caspian.

"Then put this mantle over all to hide the sword and the wallet. That's right. And now we must go to the Great Tower and talk."

When they had reached the top of the Tower (it was a cloudy night, not at all like the night when they had seen the conjunction of Tarva and Alambil) Doctor Cornelius said,

"Dear Prince, you must leave this castle at once and go to seek your fortune in the wide world. Your life is in danger here."

"Why?" asked Caspian.

"Because you are the true King of Narnia: Caspian the Tenth, the true son and heir of Caspian the Ninth. Long life to your Majesty' – and suddenly, to Caspian's great surprise, the little man dropped down on one knee and kissed his hand.

"What does it all mean? I don't understand," said Caspian.

"I wonder you have never asked me before," said the Doctor, "why, being the son of King Caspian, you are not King Caspian yourself. Everyone except your Majesty knows that Miraz is a usurper. When he first began to rule he did not even pretend to be the King: he called himself Lord Protector. But then your royal mother died, the good Queen and the only Telmarine who was ever kind to me. And then, one by one, all the great lords, who had known your father, died or disappeared. Not by accident, either. Miraz weeded them out. Belisar and Uvilas were shot with arrows on a hunting party: by chance, it was pretended. All the great house of the Passarids he sent to fight giants on the northern frontier till one by one they fell. Arlian and Erimon and a dozen more he executed for treason on a false charge. The two brothers of Beaversdam he shut up as madmen. And finally he persuaded the seven noble lords, who alone among all the Telmarines did not fear the sea, to sail away and look for new lands beyond the Eastern Ocean, and, as he intended, they never came back. And when there was no one left who could speak a word for you, then his flatterers (as he had instructed them) begged him to become King. And of course he did."

"Do you mean he now wants to kill me too?" said Caspian.

"That is almost certain," said Doctor Cornelius.

"But why now?" said Caspian. "I mean, why didn't he do it long ago if he wanted to? And what harm have I done him?"

"He has changed his mind about you because of something that happened only two hours ago. The Queen has had a son."

"I don't see what that's got to do with it," said Caspian.

"Don't see!" exclaimed the Doctor. "Have all my lessons in History and Politics taught you no more than that? Listen. As long as he had no children of his own, he was willing enough that you should be King after he died. He may not have cared much about you, but he would rather you should have the throne than a stranger. Now that he has a son of his own he will want his own son to be the next King. You are in the way. He'll clear you out of the way."

"Is he really as bad as that?" said Caspian. "Would he really murder me?"

"He murdered your Father," said Doctor Cornelius.

Caspian felt very queer and said nothing.

"I can tell you the whole story," said the Doctor. "But not now. There is no time. You must fly at once."

"You'll come with me?" said Caspian.

"I dare not," said the Doctor. "It would make your

danger greater. Two are more easily tracked than one. Dear Prince, dear King Caspian, you must be very brave. You must go alone and at once. Try to get across the southern border to the court of King Nain of Archenland. He will be good to you."

"Shall I never see you again?" said Caspian in a quavering voice.

"I hope so, dear King," said the Doctor. "What friend have I in the wide world except your Majesty? And I have a little magic. But in the meantime, speed is everything. Here are two gifts before you go. This is a little purse of gold – alas, all the treasure in this castle should be your own by rights. And here is something far better."

He put in Caspian's hands something which he could hardly see but which he knew by the feel to be a horn.

"That," said Doctor Cornelius, "is the greatest and most sacred treasure of Narnia. Many terrors I endured, many spells did I utter, to find it, when I was still young. It is the magic horn of Queen Susan herself which she left behind her when she vanished from Narnia at the end of the Golden Age. It is said that whoever blows it shall have strange help – no one can say how strange. It may have the power to call Queen Lucy and King Edmund and Queen Susan and High King Peter back from the past, and they will set all to rights. It may be that it will call up Aslan himself. Take it, King Caspian: but do not use it except at your greatest need. And now, haste, haste, haste. The little door at the very bottom of the Tower, the door into the garden, is unlocked. There we must part."

"Can I get my horse Destrier?" said Caspian.

"He is already saddled and waiting for you just at the corner of the orchard."

During the long climb down the winding staircase Cornelius whispered many more words of direction and advice. Caspian's heart was sinking, but he tried to take it all in. Then came the fresh air in the garden, a fervent handclasp with the Doctor, a run across the lawn, a welcoming whinny from Destrier, and so King Caspian the Tenth left the castle of his fathers. Looking back, he saw fireworks going up to celebrate the birth of the new prince.

All night he rode southward, choosing by-ways and bridle paths through woods as long as he was in country that he knew; but afterwards he kept to the high road. Destrier was as excited as his master at this unusual journey, and Caspian, though tears had come into his eyes at saying good-bye to Doctor Cornelius, felt brave and, in a way, happy, to think that he was King Caspian riding to seek adventures, with his sword on his left hip and Queen Susan's magic horn on his right. But when day came, with a sprinkle of rain, and he looked about him and saw on every side unknown woods, wild heaths, and blue mountains, he thought how large and strange the world was and felt frightened and small.

As soon as it was full daylight he left the road and found an open grassy place amid a wood where he could rest. He took off Destrier's bridle and let him graze, ate some cold chicken and drank a little wine, and presently fell asleep. It was late afternoon when he awoke. He ate a morsel and continued his journey, still southward, by many unfrequented lanes. He was now in a land of hills, going up and down, but always more up than down. From every ridge he could see the mountains growing bigger and blacker ahead. As the evening closed in, he was riding their lower slopes. The wind rose. Soon rain fell in torrents.

Destrier became uneasy; there was thunder in the air. And now they entered a dark and seemingly endless pine forest, and all the stories Caspian had ever heard of trees being unfriendly to Man crowded into his mind. He remembered that he was, after all, a Telmarine, one of the race who cut down trees wherever they could and were at war with all wild things; and though he himself might be

unlike other Telmarines, the trees could not be expected to know this.

Nor did they. The wind became a tempest, the woods roared and creaked all round them. There came a crash. A tree fell right across the road just behind him. "Quiet, Destrier, quiet!" said Caspian, patting his horse's neck; but he was trembling himself and knew that he had escaped death by an inch. Lightning flashed and a great crack of thunder seemed to break the sky in two just overhead.

Destrier bolted in good earnest. Caspian was a good rider, but he had not the strength to hold him back. He kept his seat, but he knew that his life hung by a thread during the wild career that followed. Tree after tree rose up before them in the dusk and was only just avoided. Then, almost too suddenly to hurt (and yet it did hurt him too) something struck Caspian on the forehead and he knew no more.

When he came to himself he was lying in a firelit place with bruised limbs and a bad headache. Low voices were speaking close at hand.

"And now," said one, "before it wakes up we must decide what to do with it."

"Kill it," said another. "We can't let it live. It would betray us."

"We ought to have killed it at once, or else let it alone," said a third voice. "We can't kill it now. Not after we've taken it in and bandaged its head and all. It would be murdering a guest."

"Gentlemen," said Caspian in a feeble voice, "whatever you do to me, I hope you will be kind to my poor horse."

"Your horse had taken flight long before we found you," said the first voice – a curiously husky, earthy voice, as Caspian now noticed.

"Now don't let it talk you round with its pretty words," said the second voice. "I still say –"

"Horns and halibuts!" exclaimed the third voice. "Of course we're not going to murder it. For shame, Nikabrik. What do you say, Trufflehunter? What shall we do with it?"

"I shall give it a drink," said the first voice, presumably

Trufflehunter's. A dark shape approached the bed. Caspian felt an arm slipped gently under his shoulders – if it was exactly an arm. The shape somehow seemed wrong. The face that bent towards him seemed wrong too. He got the impression that it was very hairy and very long nosed, and there were odd white patches on each side of it. "It's a mask of some sort," thought Caspian. "Or perhaps I'm in a fever and imagining it all." A cupful of something sweet and hot was set to his lips and he drank. At that moment one of the others poked the fire. A blaze sprang up and Caspian almost screamed with the shock as the sudden light revealed the face that was looking into his own. It was not a man's face but a badger's, though larger and friendlier and more intelligent than the face of any badger he had seen before. And it had certainly been talking. He saw, too, that he was on a bed of heather, in a cave. By the fire sat two little bearded men, so much wilder and shorter and hairier and thicker than Doctor Cornelius that he knew them at once for real Dwarfs, ancient Dwarfs with not a drop of human blood in their veins. And Caspian knew that he had found the Old Narnians at last. Then his head began to swim again.

In the next few days he learned to know them by names.

The Badger was called Trufflehunter; he was the oldest and kindest of the three. The Dwarf who had wanted to kill Caspian was a sour Black Dwarf (that is, his hair and beard were black, and thick and hard like horse-hair). His name was Nikabrik. The other Dwarf was a Red Dwarf with hair rather like a Fox's and he was called Trumpkin.

"And now," said Nikabrik on the first evening when Caspian was well enough to sit up and talk, "we still have to decide what to do with this Human. You two think you've done it a great kindess by not letting me kill it. But I suppose the upshot is that we have to keep it a prisoner for life. I'm certainly not going to let it go alive – to go back to its own kind and betray us all."

"Bulbs and bolsters! Nikabrik," said Trumpkin. "Why need you talk so unhandsomely? It isn't the creature's fault that it bashed its head against a tree outside our hole. And I don't think it looks like a traitor."

"I say," said Caspian, "you haven't yet found out whether I *want* to go back. I don't. I want to stay with you – if you'll let me. I've been looking for people like you all my life."

"That's a likely story," growled Nikabrik. "You're a Telmarine and a Human, aren't you? Of course you want to go back to your own kind."

"Well, even if I did, I couldn't," said Caspian. "I was flying for my life when I had my accident. The King wants to kill me. If you'd killed me, you'd have done the very thing to please him."

"Well now," said Trufflehunter, "you don't say so!"

"Eh?" said Trumpkin. "What's that? What have you been doing, Human, to fall foul of Miraz at your age?"

"He's my uncle," began Caspian, when Nikabrik jumped up with his hand on his dagger.

"There you are!" he cried. "Not only a Telmarine but close kin and heir to our greatest enemy. Are you still mad enough to let this creature live?" He would have stabbed Caspian then and there, if the Badger and Trumpkin had not got in the way and forced him back to his seat and held him down.

"Now, once and for all, Nikabrik," said Trumpkin. "Will you contain yourself, or must Trufflehunter and I sit on your head?"

Nikabrik sulkily promised to behave, and the other two asked Caspian to tell his whole story. When he had done so there was a moment's silence.

"This is the queerest thing I ever heard," said Trumpkin.

"I don't like it," said Nikabrik. "I didn't know there were stories about us still told among the Humans. The less they know about us the better. That old nurse, now. She'd better have held her tongue. And it's all mixed up with that Tutor: a renegade Dwarf. I hate 'em. I hate 'em worse than the Humans. You mark my words – no good will come of it."

"Don't you go talking about things you don't understand, Nikabrik," said Trufflehunter. "You Dwarfs are as forgetful and changeable as the Humans themselves. I'm a beast, I am, and a Badger what's more. We don't change. We hold on. I say great good will come of it. This is the true King of Narnia we've got here: a true King, coming back to true Narnia. And we beasts remember, even if Dwarfs forget, that Narnia was never right except when a son of Adam was King."

"Whistles and whirligigs! Trufflehunter," said

Trumpkin. "You don't mean you want to give the country to Humans?"

"I said nothing about that," answered the Badger. "It's not Men's country (who should know that better than me?) but it's a country for a man to be King of. We badgers have long enough memories to know that. Why, bless us all, wasn't the High King Peter a Man?"

"Do you believe all those old stories?" asked Trumpkin.

"I tell you, we don't change, we beasts," said Trufflehunter. "We don't forget. I believe in the High King Peter and the rest that reigned at Cair Paravel, as firmly as I believe in Aslan himself."

"As firmly as *that*, I dare say," said Trumpkin. "But who believes in Aslan nowadays?"

"I do," said Caspian. "And if I hadn't believed in him before, I would now. Back there among the Humans the people who laughed at Aslan would have laughed at stories about Talking Beasts and Dwarfs. Sometimes I did wonder if there really was such a person as Aslan: but then sometimes I wondered if there were really people like you. Yet there you are."

"That's right," said Trufflehunter. "You're right, King Caspian. And as long as you will be true to Old Narnia you shall be *my* King, whatever they say. Long life to your Majesty."

"You make me sick, Badger," growled Nikabrik. "The High King Peter and the rest may have been Men, but they were a different sort of Men. This is one of the cursed Telmarines. He has *hunted* beasts for sport. Haven't you, now?" he added, rounding suddenly on Caspian.

"Well, to tell you the truth, I have," said Caspian. "But they weren't Talking Beasts."

"It's all the same thing," said Nikabrik.

"No, no, no," said Trufflehunter. "You know it isn't. You know very well that the beasts in Narnia nowadays are different and are no more than the poor dumb, witless creatures you'd find in Calormen or Telmar. They're smaller too. They're far more different from us than the half-Dwarfs are from you."

There was a great deal more talk, but it all ended with the agreement that Caspian should stay and even the promise that, as soon as he was able to go out, he should be taken to see what Trumpkin called "the Others"; for apparently in these wild parts all sorts of creatures from the Old Days of Narnia still lived on in hiding.

CHAPTER SIX

THE PEOPLE THAT LIVED IN HIDING

Now began the happiest times that Caspian had ever known. On a fine summer morning when the dew lay on the grass he set off with the Badger and the two Dwarfs, up through the forest to a high saddle in the mountains and down on to their sunny southern slopes where one looked across the green wolds of Archenland.

"We will go first to the Three Bulgy Bears," said Trumpkin.

They came in a glade to an old hollow oak tree covered with moss, and Trufflehunter tapped with his paw three times on the trunk and there was no answer. Then he tapped again and a woolly sort of voice from inside said, "Go away. It's not time to get up yet." But when he tapped the third time there was a noise like a small earthquake from inside and a sort of door opened and out came three brown bears, very bulgy indeed and blinking their little eyes. And when everything had been explained to them (which took a long time because they were so sleepy) they said, just as Trufflehunter had said, that a son of Adam ought to be King of Narnia and all kissed Caspian – very wet, snuffly kisses they were – and offered him some honey. Caspian did not really want honey, without bread, at that time in the morning, but he thought it polite to accept. It took him a long time afterwards to get unsticky.

After that they went on till they came among tall beech trees and Trufflehunter called out, "Pattertwig! Pattertwig! Pattertwig!" and almost at once, bounding down from branch to branch till he was just above their heads, came

the most magnificent red squirrel that Caspian had ever seen. He was far bigger than the ordinary dumb squirrels which he had sometimes seen in the castle gardens; indeed he was nearly the size of a terrier and the moment you looked in his face you saw that he could talk. Indeed the difficulty was to get him to stop talking, for, like all squirrels, he was a chatterer. He welcomed Caspian at once and asked if he would like a nut and Caspian said thanks, he would. But as Pattertwig went bounding away to fetch it, Trufflehunter whispered in Caspian's ear, "Don't look. Look the other way. It's very bad manners among squirrels to watch anyone going to his store or to look as if you wanted to know where it was." Then Pattertwig came back with the nut and Caspian ate it and after that Pattertwig asked if he could take any messages to other friends. "For I can go nearly everywhere without setting foot to ground," he said. Trufflehunter and the Dwarfs thought this a very good idea and gave Pattertwig messages to all sorts of people with queer names telling them all to come to a feast and council on Dancing Lawn at midnight three nights ahead. "And you'd better tell the three Bulgies too," added Trumpkin. "We forgot to mention it to them."

Their next visit was to the Seven Brothers of Shuddering

Wood. Trumpkin led the way back to the saddle and then down eastward on the northern slope of the mountains till they came to a very solemn place among rocks and fir trees. They went very quietly and presently Caspian could feel the ground shake under his feet as if someone were hammering down below. Trumpkin went to a flat stone about the size of the top of a water-butt, and stamped on it with his foot. After a long pause it was moved away by someone or something underneath, and there was a dark, round hole with a good deal of heat and steam coming out of it and in the middle of the hole the head of a Dwarf very like Trumpkin himself. There was a long talk here and the dwarf seemed more suspicious than the Squirrel or the Bulgy Bears had been, but in the end the whole party were invited to come down. Caspian found himself descending a dark stairway into the earth, but when he came to the bottom he saw firelight. It was the light of a furnace. The whole place was a smithy. A subterranean stream ran past on one side of it. Two Dwarfs were at the bellows, another was holding a piece of red-hot metal on the anvil with a pair of tongs, a fourth was hammering it, and two, wiping their horny little hands on a greasy cloth, were coming forward to meet the visitors. It took some time to satisfy them that Caspian was a friend and not an enemy, but when they did, they all cried, "Long live the King," and their gifts were noble – mail shirts and helmets and swords for Caspian and Trumpkin and Nikabrik. The Badger could have had the same if he had liked, but he said he was a beast, he was, and if his claws and teeth could not keep his skin whole, it wasn't worth keeping. The workmanship of the arms was far finer than any Caspian had ever seen, and he gladly accepted the Dwarf-made sword instead of his own, which looked, in comparison, as feeble as a toy and as clumsy as a stick. The seven brothers (who were all Red Dwarfs) promised to come to the feast at Dancing Lawn.

A little farther on, in a dry, rocky ravine they reached the cave of five Black Dwarfs. They looked suspiciously at Caspian, but in the end the eldest of them said, "If he is against Miraz, we'll have him for King." And the next oldest said, "Shall we go farther up for you, up to the crags? There's an Ogre or two and a Hag that we could introduce you to, up there."

"Certainly not," said Caspian.

"I should think not, indeed," said Trufflehunter. "We want none of that sort on our side." Nikabrik disagreed with this, but Trumpkin and the Badger overruled him. It gave Caspian a shock to realize that the horrible creatures out of the old stories, as well as the nice ones, had some descendants in Narnia still.

"We should not have Aslan for friend if we brought in *that* rabble," said Trufflehunter as they came away from the cave of the Black Dwarfs.

"Oh, Aslan!" said Trumpkin, cheerily but contemptuously. "What matters much more is that you wouldn't have me."

"Do *you* believe in Aslan?" said Caspian to Nikabrik.

"I'll believe in anyone or anything," said Nikabrik, "that'll batter these cursed Telmarine barbarians to pieces or drive them out of Narnia. Anyone or anything, Aslan *or* the White Witch, do you understand?"

"Silence, silence," said Trufflehunter. "You do not know what you are saying. She was a worse enemy than Miraz and all his race."

"Not to Dwarfs, she wasn't," said Nikabrik.

Their next visit was a pleasanter one. As they came lower down, the mountains opened out into a great glen or wooded gorge with a swift river running at the bottom. The open places near the river's edge were a mass of foxgloves and wild roses and the air was buzzing with bees. Here Trufflehunter called again, "Glenstorm! Glenstorm!" and after a pause Caspian heard the sound of hoofs. It grew louder till the valley trembled and at last, breaking and trampling the thickets, there came in sight the noblest creatures that Caspian had yet seen, the great Centaur Glenstorm and his three sons. His flanks were glossy chestnut and the beard that covered his broad chest was golden-red. He was a prophet and a star-gazer and knew what they had come about.

"Long live the King," he cried. "I and my sons are ready for war. When is the battle to be joined?"

Up till now neither Caspian nor the others had really been thinking of a war. They had some vague idea, perhaps, of an occasional raid on some Human farmstead or of attacking a party of hunters, if it ventured too far into these southern wilds. But, in the main, they had thought only of living to themselves in woods and caves and building up an attempt at Old Narnia in hiding. As soon as Glenstorm had spoken everyone felt much more serious.

"Do you mean a real war to drive Miraz out of Narnia?" asked Caspian.

"What else?" said the Centaur. "Why else does your Majesty go clad in mail and girt with sword?"

"Is it possible, Glenstorm?" said the Badger.

"The time is ripe," said Glenstorm. "I watch the skies,

Badger, for it is mine to watch, as it is yours to remember, Tarva and Alambil have met in the halls of high heaven, and on earth a son of Adam has once more arisen to rule and name the creatures. The hour has struck. Our council at the Dancing Lawn must be a council of war." He spoke in such a voice that neither Caspian nor the others hesitated for a moment: it now seemed to them quite possible that they might win a war and quite certain that they must wage one.

As it was now past the middle of the day, they rested with the Centaurs and ate such food as the centaurs provided – cakes of oaten meal, and apples, and herbs, and wine, and cheese.

The next place they were to visit was quite near at hand, but they had to go a long way round in order to avoid a region in which Men lived. It was well into the afternoon before they found themselves in level fields, warm between hedgerows. There Trufflehunter called at the mouth of a little hole in a green bank and out popped the last thing Caspian expected – a Talking Mouse. He was of course bigger than a common mouse, well over a foot high when he stood on his hind legs, and with ears nearly as long as (though broader than) a rabbit's. His name was Reepicheep and he was a gay and martial mouse. He wore a tiny little rapier at his side and twirled his long whiskers as if they were a moustache. "There are twelve of us, Sire," he said with a dashing and graceful bow, "and I place all the resources of my people unreservedly at your Majesty's disposal." Caspian tried hard (and successfully) not to laugh, but he couldn't help thinking that Reepicheep and all his people could very easily be put in a washing basket and carried home on one's back.

It would take too long to mention all the creatures whom Caspian met that day – Clodsley Shovel the Mole, the three Hardbiters (who were badgers like Trufflehunter), Camillo the Hare, and Hogglestock the Hedgehog. They rested at last beside a well at the edge of a wide and level circle of grass, bordered with tall elms which now threw long shadows across it, for the sun was setting, the daisies closing, and the rooks flying home to bed. Here they supped on food they had brought with them and Trumpkin lit his pipe (Nikabrik was not a smoker).

"Now," said the Badger, "if only we could wake the spirits of these trees and this well, we should have done a good day's work."

"Can't we?" said Caspian.

"No," said Trufflehunter. "We have no power over them. Since the Humans came into the land, felling forests and defiling streams, the Dryads and Naiads have sunk into a deep sleep. Who knows if ever they will stir again? And that is a great loss to our side. The Telmarines are horribly afraid of the woods, and once the Trees moved in anger, our enemies would go mad with fright and be chased out of Narnia as quick as their legs could carry them."

"What imaginations you Animals have!" said Trumpkin, who didn't believe in such things. "But why stop at Trees and Waters? Wouldn't it be even nicer if the stones started throwing themselves at old Miraz?"

The Badger only grunted at this, and after that there was such a silence that Caspian had nearly dropped off to sleep

when he thought he heard a faint musical sound from the depth of the woods at his back. Then he thought it was only a dream and turned over again; but as soon as his ear touched the ground he felt or heard (it was hard to tell which) a faint beating or drumming. He raised his head. The beating noise at once became fainter, but the music returned, clearer this time. It was like flutes. He saw that Trufflehunter was sitting up staring into the wood. The moon was bright; Caspian had been asleep longer than he thought. Nearer and nearer came the music, a tune wild and yet dreamy, and the noise of many light feet, till at last, out from the wood into the moonlight, came dancing shapes such as Caspian had been thinking of all his life. They were not much taller than dwarfs, but far slighter and more graceful. Their curly heads had little horns, the upper part of their bodies gleamed naked in the pale light, but their legs and feet were those of goats.

"Fauns!" cried Caspian, jumping up, and in a moment they were all round him. It took next to no time to explain the whole situation to them and they accepted Caspian at once. Before he knew what he was doing he found himself joining in the dance. Trumpkin, with heavier and jerkier movements, did likewise and even Trufflehunter hopped and lumbered about as best he could. Only Nikabrik stayed where he was, looking on in silence. The Fauns footed it all round Caspian to their reedy pipes. Their strange faces, which seemed mournful and merry all at once, looked into his; dozens of Fauns, Mentius and Obentinus and Dumnus, Voluns, Voltinus, Girbius, Nimienus, Nausus, and Oscuns. Pattertwig had sent them all.

When Caspian awoke next morning he could hardly believe that it had not all been a dream; but the grass was covered with little cloven hoof-marks.

CHAPTER SEVEN

OLD NARNIA IN DANGER

THE place where they had met the Fauns was, of course, Dancing Lawn itself, and here Caspian and his friends remained till the night of the great Council. To sleep under the stars, to drink nothing but well water and to live chiefly on nuts and wild fruit, was a strange experience for Caspian after his bed with silken sheets in a tapestried chamber at the castle, with meals laid out on gold and silver dishes in the anteroom, and attendants ready at his call. But he had never enjoyed himself more. Never had sleep been more refreshing nor food tasted more savoury, and he began already to harden and his face wore a kinglier look.

When the great night came, and his various strange subjects came stealing into the lawn by ones and twos and threes or by sixes and sevens – the moon then shining almost at her full – his heart swelled as he saw their numbers and heard their greetings. All whom he had met were there: Bulgy Bears and Red Dwarfs and Black Dwarfs, Moles and Badgers, Hares and Hedgehogs, and others whom he had not yet seen – five Satyrs as red as foxes, the whole contingent of Talking Mice, armed to the teeth and following a shrill trumpet, some Owls, the Old Raven of Ravenscaur. Last of all (and this took Caspian's breath away), with the Centaurs came a small but genuine Giant, Wimbleweather of Deadman's Hill, carrying on his back a basketful of rather sea-sick Dwarfs who had accepted his offer of a lift and were now wishing they had walked instead.

The Bulgy Bears were very anxious to have the feast first and leave the council till afterwards: perhaps till tomorrow. Reepicheep and his Mice said that councils and feasts could both wait, and proposed storming Miraz in his own castle that very night. Pattertwig and the other Squirrels said they could talk and eat at the same time, so why not have the council and feast all at once? The Moles proposed throwing up entrenchments round the Lawn before they did anything else. The Fauns thought it would be better to begin with a solemn dance. The Old Raven, while agreeing with the Bears that it would take too long to have a full council before supper, begged to be allowed to give a brief address to the whole company. But Caspian and the Centaurs and the Dwarfs overruled all these suggestions and insisted on holding a real council of war at once.

When all the other creatures had been persuaded to sit down quietly in a great circle, and when (with more difficulty) they had got Pattertwig to stop running to and fro and saying "Silence! Silence, everyone, for the King's speech", Caspian, feeling a little nervous, got up. "Narnians!" he began, but he never got any further, for at that very moment Camillo the Hare said, "Hush! There's a Man somewhere near."

They were all creatures of the wild, accustomed to being hunted, and they all became still as statues. The beasts all turned their noses in the direction which Camillo had indicated.

"Smells like Man and yet not quite like Man," whispered Trufflehunter.

"It's getting steadily nearer," said Camillo.

"Two badgers and you three Dwarfs, with your

bows at the ready, go softly off to meet it," said Caspian.

"We'll settle 'un," said a Black Dwarf grimly, fitting a shaft to his bowstring.

"Don't shoot if it is alone," said Caspian. "Catch it."

"Why?" asked the Dwarf.

"Do as you're told," said Glenstorm the Centaur.

Everyone waited in silence while the three Dwarfs and two Badgers trotted stealthily across to the trees on the north-west side of the Lawn. Then came a sharp dwarfish cry, "Stop! Who goes there?" and a sudden spring. A moment later a voice, which Caspian knew well, could he heard saying, "All right, all right, I'm unarmed. Take my wrists if you like, worthy Badgers, but don't bite right through them. I want to speak to the King."

"Doctor Cornelius!" cried Caspian with joy, and rushed forward to greet his old tutor. Everyone else crowded round.

"Pah!" said Nikabrik. "A renegade Dwarf. A half-and-halfer! Shall I pass my sword through its throat?"

"Be quiet, Nikabrik," said Trumpkin. "The creature can't help its ancestry."

"This is my greatest friend and the saviour of my life," said Caspian. "And anyone who doesn't like his company may leave my army: at once. Dearest doctor, I *am* glad to see you again. How ever did you find us out?"

"By a little use of simple magic, your Majesty," said the Doctor, who was still puffing and blowing from having walked so fast. "But there's no time to go into that now. We must all fly from this place at once. You are already betrayed and Miraz is on the move. Before midday to-morrow you will be surrounded."

"Betrayed!" said Caspian. "And by whom?"

"Another renegade Dwarf, no doubt," said Nikabrik.

"By your horse Destrier," said Doctor Cornelius. "The poor brute knew no better. When you were knocked off, of course, he went dawdling back to his stable in the castle. Then the secret of your flight was known. I made myself scarce, having no wish to be questioned about it in Miraz's torture chamber. I had a pretty good guess from my crystal as to where I should find you. But all day – that was the day before yesterday – I saw Miraz's tracking parties out in the woods. Yesterday I learned that his army is out. I don't think some of your – um – pure-blooded Dwarfs have as much woodcraft as might be expected. You've left tracks all over the place. Great carelessness. At any rate something has warned Miraz that Old Narnia is not so dead as he had hoped, and he is on the move."

"Hurrah!" said a very shrill and small voice from somewhere at the Doctor's feet. "Let them come! All I ask is that the King will put me and my people in the front."

"What on earth?" said Doctor Cornelius. "Has your Majesty got grasshoppers – or mosquitoes – in your army?" Then after stooping down and peering carefully through his spectacles, he broke into a laugh.

"By the Lion," he swore, "it's a mouse. Signior Mouse, I desire your better acquaintance. I am honoured by meeting so valiant a beast."

"My friendship you shall have, learned Man," piped Reepicheep. "And any Dwarf – or Giant – in the army who does not give you good language shall have my sword to reckon with."

"Is there time for this foolery?" asked Nikabrik. "What are our plans? Battle or flight?"

"Battle if need be," said Trumpkin. "But we are hardly ready for it yet, and this is no very defensible place."

"I don't like the idea of running away," said Caspian.

"Hear him! Hear him!" said the Bulgy Bears. "Whatever we do, don't let's have any *running*. Especially not before supper; and not too soon after it neither."

"Those who run first do not always run last," said the Centaur. "And why should we let the enemy choose our position instead of choosing it ourselves? Let us find a strong place."

"That's wise, your Majesty, that's wise," said Trufflehunter.

"But where are we to go?" asked several voices.

"Your Majesty," said Doctor Cornelius, "and all you variety of creatures, I think we must fly east and down the river to the great woods. The Telmarines hate that region. They have always been afraid of the sea and of something that may come over the sea. That is why they have let the great woods grow up. If traditions speak true, the ancient Cair Paravel was at the river-mouth. All that part is friendly to us and hateful to our enemies. We must go to Aslan's How."

"Aslan's How?" said several voices. "We do not know what it is."

"It lies within the skirts of the Great Woods and it is a huge mound which Narnians raised in very ancient times over a very magical place, where there stood – and perhaps still stands – a very magical Stone. The Mound is all hollowed out within into galleries and caves, and the Stone is in the central cave of all. There is room in the mound for all our stores, and those of us who have most need of cover and are most accustomed to underground life can be lodged in the caves. The rest of us can lie in the wood. At a pinch all of us (except this worthy Giant) could retreat into the Mound itself, and there we should be beyond the reach of every danger except famine."

"It is a good thing we have a learned man among us," said Trufflehunter; but Trumpkin muttered under his breath, "Soup and celery! I wish our leaders would think less about these old wives' tales and more about victuals and arms." But all approved of Cornelius's proposal and

that very night, half an hour later, they were on the march. Before sunrise they arrived at Aslan's How.

It was certainly an awesome place, a round green hill on top of another hill, long since grown over with trees, and one little, low doorway leading into it. The tunnels inside were a perfect maze till you got to know them, and they were lined and roofed with smooth stones, and on the stones, peering in the twilight, Caspian saw strange characters and snaky patterns, and pictures in which the form of a Lion was repeated again and again. It all seemed to belong to an even older Narnia than the Narnia of which his nurse had told him.

It was after they had taken up their quarters in and around the How that fortune began to turn against them. King Miraz's scouts soon found their new lair, and he and his army arrived on the edge of the woods. And as so often happens, the enemy turned out stronger than they had reckoned. Caspian's heart sank as he saw company after company arriving. And though Miraz's men may have been afraid of going into the wood, they were even more afraid of Miraz, and with him in command they carried battle deeply into it and sometimes almost to the How itself. Caspian and other captains of course made many sorties into the open country. Thus there was fighting on most days and sometimes by night as well; but Caspian's party had on the whole the worst of it.

At last there came a night when everything had gone as badly as possible, and the rain which had been falling heavily all day had ceased at nightfall only to give place to raw cold. That morning Caspian had arranged what was his biggest battle yet, and all had hung their hopes on it. He, with most of the Dwarfs, was to have fallen on the King's right wing at daybreak, and then, when they were heavily engaged, Giant Wimbleweather, with the Centaurs and some of the fiercest beasts, was to have broken out from another place and endeavoured to cut the King's right off from the rest of the army. But it had all failed. No one had warned Caspian (because no one in these later days of Narnia remembered) that Giants are not at all clever. Poor Wimbleweather, though as brave as a lion, was a true Giant in that respect. He had broken out at the wrong time and from the wrong place, and both his party and

Caspian's had suffered badly and done the enemy little harm. The best of the Bears had been hurt, a Centaur terribly wounded, and there were few in Caspian's party who had not lost blood. It was a gloomy company that huddled under the dripping trees to eat their scanty supper.

The gloomiest of all was Giant Wimbleweather. He knew it was all his fault. He sat in silence shedding big tears which collected on the end of his nose and then fell off with a huge splash on the whole bivouac of the Mice, who had just been beginning to get warm and drowsy. They all jumped up, shaking the water out of their ears and wringing their little blankets, and asked the Giant in shrill but forcible voices whether he thought they weren't wet enough without this sort of thing. And then other people woke up and told the Mice they had been enrolled as scouts and not as a concert party, and asked why they

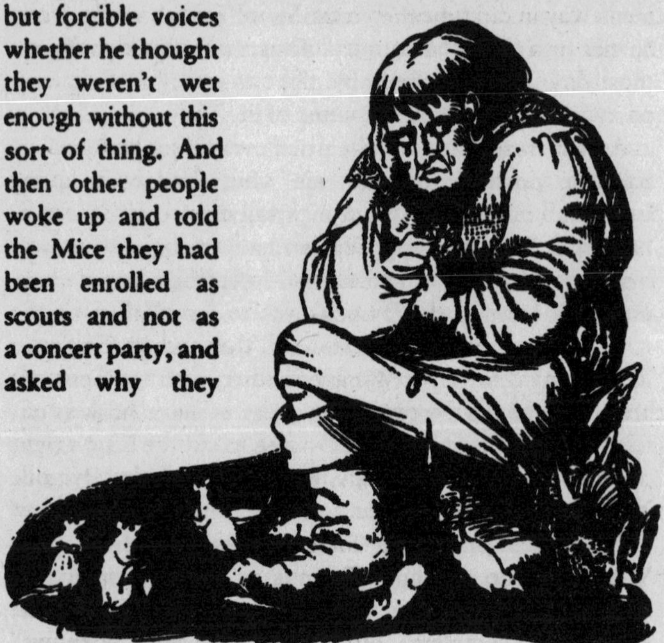

couldn't keep quiet. And Wimbleweather tiptoed away to find some place where he could be miserable in peace and stepped on somebody's tail and somebody (they said afterwards it was a fox) bit him. And so everyone was out of temper.

But in the secret and magical chamber at the heart of the How, King Caspian, with Cornelius and the Badger and Nikabrik and Trumpkin, were at council. Thick pillars of ancient workmanship supported the roof. In the centre was the Stone itself – a stone table, split right down the centre, and covered with what had once been writing of some kind: but ages of wind and rain and snow had almost worn them away in old times when the Stone Table had stood on the hilltop, and the Mound had not yet been built above it. They were not using the Table nor sitting round it: it was too magic a thing for any common use. They sat on logs a little way from it, and between them was a rough wooden table, on which stood a rude clay lamp lighting up their pale faces and throwing big shadows on the walls.

"If your Majesty is ever to use the Horn," said Trufflehunter, "I think the time has now come." Caspian had of course told them of his treasure several days ago.

"We are certainly in great need," answered Caspian. "But it is hard to be sure we are at our greatest. Supposing there came an even worse need and we had already used it?"

"By that argument," said Nikabrik, "your Majesty will never use it until it is too late."

"I agree with that," said Doctor Cornelius.

"And what do you think, Trumpkin?" asked Caspian.

"Oh, as for me," said the Red Dwarf, who had been listening with complete indifference, "your Majesty knows

I think the Horn – and that bit of broken stone over there – and your great King Peter – and your Lion Aslan – are all eggs in moonshine. It's all one to me when your Majesty blows the Horn. All I insist on is that the army is told nothing about it. There's no good raising hopes of magical help which (as I think) are sure to be disappointed."

"Then in the name of Aslan we will wind Queen Susan's Horn," said Caspian.

"There is one thing, Sire," said Doctor Cornelius, "that should perhaps be done first. We do not know what form the help will take. It might call Aslan himself from oversea. But I think it is more likely to call Peter the High King and his mighty consorts down from the high past. But in either case, I do not think we can be sure that the help will come to this very spot –"

"You never said a truer word," put in Trumpkin.

"I think," went on the learned man, "that they – or he – will come back to one or other of the Ancient Places of Narnia. This, where we now sit, is the most ancient and most deeply magical of all, and here, I think, the answer is likeliest to come. But there are two others. One is Lantern Waste, up-river, west of Beaversdam, where the Royal Children first appeared in Narnia, as the records tell. The other is down at the river-mouth, where their castle of Cair Paravel once stood. And if Aslan himself comes, that would be the best place for meeting him too, for every story says that he is the son of the great Emperor-over-the-Sea, and over the sea he will pass. I should like very much to send messengers to both places, to Lantern Waste and the river-mouth, to receive them – or him – or it."

"Just as I thought," muttered Trumpkin. "The first

result of all this foolery is not to bring us help but to lose us two fighters."

"Who would you think of sending, Doctor Cornelius?" asked Caspian.

"Squirrels are best for getting through enemy country without being caught," said Trufflehunter.

"All *our* squirrels (and we haven't many)," said Nikabrik, "are rather flighty. The only one I'd trust on a job like that would be Pattertwig."

"Let it be Pattertwig, then," said King Caspian. "And who for our other messenger? I know you'd go, Trufflehunter, but you haven't the speed. Nor you, Doctor Cornelius."

"I *won't* go," said Nikabrik. "With all these Humans and beasts about, there must be a Dwarf here to see that the Dwarfs are fairly treated."

"Thimbles and thunderstorms!" cried Trumpkin in a rage. "Is that how you speak to the King? Send me, Sire, I'll go."

"But I thought you didn't believe in the Horn, Trumpkin," said Caspian.

"No more I do, your Majesty. But what's that got to do with it? I might as well die on a wild goose chase as die here. You are my King. I know the difference between giving advice and taking orders. You've had my advice, and now it's the time for orders."

"I will never forget this, Trumpkin," said Caspian. "Send for Pattertwig, one of you. And when shall I blow the Horn?"

"I would wait for sunrise, your Majesty," said Doctor Cornelius. "That sometimes has an effect in operations of White Magic."

A few minutes later Pattertwig arrived and had his task explained to him. As he was, like many squirrels, full of courage and dash and energy and excitement and mischief (not to say conceit), he no sooner heard it than he was eager to be off. It was arranged that he should run for Lantern Waste while Trumpkin made the shorter journey to the river-mouth. After a hasty meal they both set off with the fervent thanks and good wishes of the King, the Badger, and Cornelius.

CHAPTER EIGHT

HOW THEY LEFT THE ISLAND

"And so," said Trumpkin (for, as you have realized, it was he who had been telling all this story to the four children, sitting on the grass in the ruined hall of Cair Paravel) – "and so I put a crust or two in my pocket, left behind all weapons but my dagger, and took to the woods in the grey of the morning. I'd been plugging away for many hours when there came a sound that I'd never heard the like of in my born days. Eh, I won't forget that. The whole air was full of it, loud as thunder but far longer, cool and sweet as music over water, but strong enough to shake the woods. And I said to myself, 'If that's not the Horn, call me a rabbit.' And a moment later I wondered why he hadn't blown it sooner –"

"What time was it?" asked Edmund.

"Between nine and ten of the clock," said Trumpkin.

"Just when we were at the railway station!" said all the children, and looked at one another with shining eyes.

"Please go on," said Lucy to the Dwarf.

"Well, as I was saying, I wondered, but I went on as hard as I could pelt. I kept on all night – and then, when it was half light this morning, as if I'd no more sense than a Giant, I risked a short cut across open country to cut off a big loop of the river, and was caught. Not by the army, but by a pompous old fool who has charge of a little castle which is Miraz's last stronghold towards the coast. I needn't tell you they got no true tale out of me, but I was a Dwarf and that was enough. But, lobsters and lollipops! it is a good thing the seneschal *was* a pompous fool. Anyone else would have run me through there and then. But nothing would do for him short of a grand execution: sending me down 'to the ghosts' in the full ceremonial way. And then this young lady" (he nodded at Susan) "does her bit of archery – and it was pretty shooting, let me tell you – and here we are. And without my armour, for of course they took that." He knocked out and refilled his pipe.

"Great Scott!" said Peter. "So it was the horn – your own horn, Su – that dragged us all off that seat on the platform yesterday morning! I can hardly believe it; yet it all fits in."

"I don't know why you shouldn't believe it," said Lucy, "if you believe in magic at all. Aren't there lots of stories about magic forcing people out of one place – out of one world – into another? I mean, when a magician in *The Arabian Nights* calls up a Jinn, it has to come. We had to come, just like that."

"Yes," said Peter, "I suppose what makes it feel so queer is that in the stories it's always someone in our world who does the calling. One doesn't really think about where the Jinn's coming *from.*"

"And now we know what it feels like for the Jinn," said Edmund with a chuckle. "Golly! It's a bit uncomfortable to know that *we* can be whistled for like that. It's worse than what Father says about living at the mercy of the telephone."

"But we want to be here, don't we," said Lucy, "if Aslan wants us?"

"Meanwhile," said the Dwarf, "what are we to do? I suppose I'd better go back to King Caspian and tell him no help has come."

"No help?" said Susan. "But it *has* worked. And here we are."

"Um – um – yes, to be sure. I see that," said the Dwarf, whose pipe seemed to be blocked (at any rate he made himself very busy cleaning it). "But – well – I mean –"

"But don't you yet see who we are?" shouted Lucy. "You *are* stupid."

"I suppose you are the four children out of the old stories," said Trumpkin. "And I'm very glad to meet you of course. And it's very interesting, no doubt. But – no offence?' – and he hesitated again.

"Do get on and say whatever you're going to say," said Edmund.

"Well, then – no offence," said Trumpkin. "But, you know, the King and Trufflehunter and Doctor Cornelius were expecting – well, if you see what I mean, help. To put it in another way, I think they'd been imagining you as great warriors. As it is – we're awfully fond of children and all that, but just at the moment, in the middle of a war – but I'm sure you understand."

"You mean you think we're no good," said Edmund, getting red in the face.

"Now pray don't be offended," interrupted the Dwarf. "I assure you, my dear little friends – "

"*Little* from you is really a bit too much," said Edmund, jumping up. "I suppose you don't believe we won the Battle of Beruna? Well, you can say what you like about me because I know –"

"There's no good losing our tempers," said Peter. "Let's fit him out with fresh armour and fit ourselves out from the treasure chamber, and have a talk after that."

"I don't quite see the point –" began Edmund, but Lucy

whispered in his ear, "Hadn't we better do what Peter says? He is the High King, you know. And I think he has an idea." So Edmund agreed and by the aid of his torch they all, including Trumpkin, went down the steps again into the dark coldness and dusty splendour of the treasure house.

The Dwarf's eyes glistened as he saw the wealth that lay on the shelves (though he had to stand on tiptoes to do so) and he muttered to himself, "It would never do to let Nikabrik see this; never." They found easily enough a mail shirt for him, a sword, a helmet, a shield, a bow and quiverful of arrows, all of dwarfish size. The helmet was of copper, set with rubies, and there was gold on the hilt of the sword: Trumpkin had never seen, much less carried, so much wealth in all his life. The children also put on mail shirts and helmets; a sword and shield were found for Edmund and a bow for Lucy – Peter and Susan were of course already carrying their gifts. As they came back up the stairway, jingling in their mail, and already looking and feeling more like Narnians and less like schoolchildren, the two boys were behind, apparently making some plan. Lucy heard Edmund say, "No, let me do it. It will be more of a sucks for him if I win, and less of a let-down for us all if I fail."

"All right, Ed," said Peter.

When they came out into the daylight Edmund turned to the Dwarf very politely and said, "I've got something to ask you. Kids like us don't often have the chance of meeting a great warrior like you. Would you have a little fencing match with me? It would be frightfully decent."

"But, lad," said Trumpkin, "these swords are sharp."

"I know," said Edmund. "But I'll never get anywhere

near you and you'll be quite clever enough to disarm me without doing me any damage."

"It's a dangerous game," said Trumpkin. "But since you make such a point of it, I'll try a pass or two."

Both swords were out in a moment and the three others jumped off the dais and stood watching. It was well worth it. It was not like the silly fighting you see with broad swords on the stage. It was not even like the rapier fighting which you sometimes see rather better done. This was real broad-sword fighting. The great thing is to slash at your enemy's legs and feet because they are the part that have no armour. And when he slashes at yours you jump with both feet off the ground so that his blow goes under them. This gave the Dwarf an advantage because Edmund, being much taller, had to be always stooping. I don't think Edmund would have had a chance if he had fought Trumpkin twenty-four hours earlier. But the air of Narnia had been working upon him ever since they arrived on the island, and all his old battles came back to him, and his arms and fingers remembered their old skill. He was King Edmund once more. Round and round the two combatants circled, stroke after stroke they gave, and Susan (who never could learn to like this sort of thing) shouted out, "Oh, *do* be careful." And then, so quickly that no one (unless they knew, as Peter did) could quite see how it happened, Edmund flashed his sword round with a peculiar twist, the Dwarf's sword flew out of his grip, and Trumpkin was wringing his empty hand as you do after a "sting" from a cricket-bat.

"Not hurt, I hope, my dear little friend?" said Edmund, panting a little and returning his own sword to its sheath.

"I see the point," said Trumpkin drily. "You know a trick I never learned."

"That's quite true," put in Peter. "The best swordsman in the world may be disarmed by a trick that's new to him. I think it's only fair to give Trumpkin a chance at something else. Will you have a shooting match with my sister? There are no tricks in archery, you know."

"Ah, you're jokers, you are," said the Dwarf. "I begin to

see. As if I didn't know how she can shoot, after what happened this morning. All the same, I'll have a try." He spoke gruffly, but his eyes brightened, for he was a famous bowman among his own people.

All five of them came out into the courtyard.

"What's to be the target?" asked Peter.

"I think that apple hanging over the wall on the branch there would do," said Susan.

"That'll do nicely, lass," said Trumpkin. "You mean the yellow one near the middle of the arch?"

"No, not that," said Susan. "The red one up above – over the battlement."

The Dwarf's face fell. "Looks more like a cherry than an apple," he muttered, but he said nothing out loud.

They tossed up for first shot (greatly to the interest of Trumpkin, who had never seen a coin tossed before) and Susan lost. They were to shoot from the top of the steps that led from the hall into the courtyard. Everyone could see from the way the Dwarf took his position and handled his bow that he knew what he was about.

Twang went the string. It was an excellent shot. The tiny apple shook as the arrow passed, and a leaf came fluttering down. Then Susan went to the top of the steps and strung her bow. She was not enjoying her match half so much as Edmund had enjoyed his; not because she had any doubt about hitting the apple but because Susan was so tender-hearted that she almost hated to beat someone who had been beaten already. The Dwarf watched her keenly as she drew the shaft to her ear. A moment later, with a little soft thump which they could all hear in that quiet place, the apple fell to the grass with Susan's arrow in it.

"Oh, well done, Su," shouted the other children.

"It wasn't really any better than yours," said Susan to the Dwarf. "I think there was a tiny breath of wind as you shot."

"No, there wasn't," said Trumpkin. "Don't tell me. I

know when I am fairly beaten. I won't even say that the scar of my last wound catches me a bit when I get my arm well back –"

"Oh, are you wounded?" asked Lucy. "Do let me look."

"It's not a sight for little girls," began Trumpkin, but then he suddenly checked himself. "There I go talking like a fool again," he said. "I suppose you're as likely to be a great surgeon as your brother was to be a great swordsman or your sister to be a great archer." He sat down on the steps and took off his hauberk and slipped down his little shirt, showing an arm hairy and muscular (in proportion) as a sailor's though not much bigger than a child's. There was a clumsy bandage on the shoulder which Lucy proceeded to unroll. Underneath, the cut looked very nasty and there was a good deal of swelling. "Oh, poor Trumpkin," said Lucy. "How horrid." Then she carefully dripped on to it one single drop of the cordial from her flask.

"Hullo. Eh? What have you done?" said Trumpkin. But however he turned his head and squinted and whisked his beard to and fro, he couldn't quite see his own shoulder. Then he felt it as well as he could, getting his arms and fingers into very difficult positions as you do when you're trying to scratch a place that is just out of reach. Then he swung his arm and raised it and tried the muscles, and finally jumped to his feet crying, "Giants and junipers! It's cured! It's as good as new." After that he burst into a great laugh and said, "Well, I've made as big a fool of myself as ever a Dwarf did. No offence, I hope? My humble duty to your Majesties all – humble duty. And thanks for my life, my cure, my breakfast – and my lesson."

The children all said it was quite all right and not to mention it.

"And now," said Peter, "if you've really decided to believe in us –"

"I have," said the Dwarf.

"It's quite clear what we have to do. We must join King Caspian at once."

"The sooner the better," said Trumpkin. "My being such a fool has already wasted about an hour."

"It's about two days' journey, the way you came," said Peter. "For us, I mean. We can't walk all day and night like you Dwarfs." Then he turned to the others. "What Trumpkin calls Aslan's How is obviously the Stone Table itself. You remember it was about half a day's march, or a little less, from there down to the Fords of Beruna –"

"Beruna's Bridge, we call it," said Trumpkin.

"There was no bridge in our time," said Peter. "And then from Beruna down to here was another day and a bit. We used to get home about teatime on the second day, going easily. Going hard, we could do the whole thing in a day and a half perhaps."

"But remember it's all woods now," said Trumpkin, "and there are enemies to dodge."

"Look here," said Edmund, "need we go by the same way that Our Dear Little Friend came?"

"No more of that, your Majesty, if you love me," said the Dwarf.

"Very well," said Edmund. "May I say our D.L.F.?"

"Oh, Edmund," said Susan. "Don't keep *on* at him like that."

"That's all right, lass – I mean your Majesty," said

Trumpkin with a chuckle. "A jibe won't raise a blister." (And after that they often called him the D.L.F. till they'd almost forgotten what it meant.)

"As I was saying," continued Edmund, "we needn't go that way. Why shouldn't we row a little south till we come to Glasswater Creek and row up it? That brings us up behind the Hill of the Stone Table, and we'll be safe while we're at sea. If we start at once, we can be at the head of Glasswater before dark, get a few hours' sleep, and be with Caspian pretty early tomorrow."

"What a thing it is to know the coast," said Trumpkin. "None of us know anything about Glasswater."

"What about food?" asked Susan.

"Oh, we'll have to do with apples," said Lucy. "Do let's get on. We've done nothing yet, and we've been here nearly two days."

"And anyway, no one's going to have my hat for a fish-basket again," said Edmund.

They used one of the raincoats as a kind of bag and put a good many apples in it. Then they all had a good long drink at the well (for they would meet no more fresh water till they landed at the head of the Creek) and went down to the boat. The children were sorry to leave Cair Paravel, which, even in ruins, had begun to feel like home again.

"The D.L.F. had better steer," said Peter, "and Ed and I will take an oar each. Half a moment, though. We'd better take off our mail: we're going to be pretty warm before we're done. The girls had better be in the bows and shout directions to the D.L.F. because he doesn't know the way. You'd better get us a fair way out to sea till we've passed the island."

And soon the green, wooded coast of the island was falling away behind them, and its little bays and headlands were beginning to look flatter, and the boat was rising and falling in the gentle swell. The sea began to grow bigger around them and, in the distance, bluer, but close round the boat it was green and bubbly. Everything smelled salt and there was no noise except the swishing of water and the clop-clop of water against the sides and the splash of the oars and the jolting noise of the rowlocks. The sun grew hot.

It was delightful for Lucy and Susan in the bows, bending over the edge and trying to get their hands in the sea which they could never quite reach. The bottom, mostly pure, pale sand but with occasional patches of purple seaweed, could be seen beneath them.

"It's like old times," said Lucy. "Do you remember our voyage to Terebinthia – and Galma – and Seven Isles – and the Lone Islands?"

"Yes," said Susan, "and our great ship the *Splendour Hyaline*, with the swan's head at her prow and the carved swan's wings coming back almost to her waist?"

"And the silken sails, and the great stern lanterns?"

"And the feasts on the poop and the musicians."

"Do you remember when we had the musicians up in the rigging playing flutes so that it sounded like music out of the sky?"

Presently Susan took over Edmund's oar and he came forward to join Lucy. They had passed the island now and stood closer in to the shore – all wooded and deserted. They would have thought it very pretty if they had not remembered the time when it was open and breezy and full of merry friends.

"Phew! This is pretty gruelling work," said Peter.

"Can't I row for a bit?" said Lucy.

"The oars are too big for you," said Peter shortly, not because he was cross but because he had no strength to spare for talking.

CHAPTER NINE

WHAT LUCY SAW

SUSAN and the two boys were bitterly tired with rowing before they rounded the last headland and began the final pull up Glasswater itself, and Lucy's head ached from the long hours of sun and the glare on the water. Even Trumpkin longed for the voyage to be over. The seat on which he sat to steer had been made for men, not Dwarfs, and his feet did not reach the floor-boards; and everyone knows how uncomfortable that is even for ten minutes. And as they all grew more tired, their spirits fell. Up till now the children had only been thinking of how to get to Caspian. Now they wondered what they would do when they found him, and how a handful of Dwarfs and woodland creatures could defeat an army of grown-up Humans.

Twilight was coming on as they rowed slowly up the windings of Glasswater Creek – a twilight which deepened as the banks drew closer together and the over-hanging trees began almost to meet overhead. It was very quiet in here as the sound of the sea died away behind them; they could even hear the trickle of the little streams that poured down from the forest into Glasswater.

They went ashore at last, far too tired to attempt lighting a fire; and even a supper of apples (though most of them felt that they never wanted to see an apple again) seemed better than trying to catch or shoot anything. After a little silent munching they all huddled down together in the moss and dead leaves between four large beech trees.

Everyone except Lucy went to sleep at once. Lucy, being far less tired, found it hard to get comfortable. Also, she had forgotten till now that all Dwarfs snore. She knew that one of the best ways of getting to sleep is to stop trying, so she opened her eyes. Through a gap in the bracken and branches she could just see a patch of water in the Creek and the sky above it. Then, with a thrill of memory, she saw again, after all those years, the bright Narnian stars. She had once known them better than the stars of our own world, because as a Queen in Narnia she had gone to bed much later than as a child in England. And there they were – at least, three of the summer constellations could be seen from where she lay: the Ship, the Hammer, and the Leopard. "Dear old Leopard," she murmured happily to herself.

Instead of getting drowsier she was getting more awake – with an odd, night-time, dreamish kind of wakefulness. The Creek was growing brighter. She knew now that the moon was on it, though she couldn't see the moon. And now she began to feel that the whole forest was coming awake like herself. Hardly knowing why she did it, she got up quickly and walked a little distance away from their bivouac.

"This is lovely," said Lucy to herself. It was cool and fresh; delicious smells were floating everywhere.

Somewhere close by she heard the twitter of a nightingale beginning to sing, then stopping, then beginning again. It was a little lighter ahead. She went towards the light and came to a place where there were fewer trees, and whole patches or pools of moonlight, but the moonlight and the shadows so mixed that you could hardly be sure where anything was or what it was. At the same moment the nightingale, satisfied at last with his tuning up, burst into full song.

Lucy's eyes began to grow accustomed to the light, and she saw the trees that were nearest her more distinctly. A great longing for the old days when the trees could talk in Narnia came over her. She knew exactly how each of these trees would talk if only she could wake them, and what sort of human form it would put on. She looked at a silver birch: it would have a soft, showery voice and would look like a slender girl, with hair blown all about her face, and fond of dancing. She looked at the oak: he would be a wizened, but hearty old man with a frizzled beard and warts on his face and hands, and hair growing out of the warts. She looked at the beech under which she was standing. Ah! – she would be the best of all. She would be a gracious goddess, smooth and stately, the lady of the wood.

"Oh, Trees, Trees, Trees," said Lucy (though she had not been intending to speak at all). "Oh, Trees, wake, wake, wake. Don't you remember it? Don't you remember *me*? Dryads and Hamadryads, come out, come to me."

Though there was not a breath of wind they all stirred about her. The rustling noise of the leaves was almost like words. The nightingale stopped singing as if to listen to it.

Lucy felt that at any moment she would begin to understand what the trees were trying to say. But the moment did not come. The rustling died away. The nightingale resumed its song. Even in the moonlight the wood looked more ordinary again. Yet Lucy had the feeling (as you sometimes have when you are trying to remember a name or a date and almost get it, but it vanishes before you really do) that she had just missed something: as if she

had spoken to the trees a split second too soon or a split second too late, or used all the right words except one, or put in one word that was just wrong.

Quite suddenly she began to feel tired. She went back to the bivouac, snuggled down between Susan and Peter, and was asleep in a few minutes.

It was a cold and cheerless waking for them all next morning, with a grey twilight in the wood (for the sun had not yet risen) and everything damp and dirty.

"Apples, heigh-ho," said Trumpkin with a rueful grin. "I must say you ancient kings and queens don't overfeed your courtiers!"

They stood up and shook themselves and looked about. The trees were thick and they could see no more than a few yards in any direction.

"I suppose your Majesties know the way all right?" said the Dwarf.

"I don't," said Susan. "I've never seen these woods in my life before. In fact I thought all along that we ought to have gone by the river."

"Then I think you might have said so at the time," answered Peter, with pardonable sharpness.

"Oh, don't take any notice of her," said Edmund. "She always is a wet blanket. You've got that pocket compass of yours, Peter, haven't you? Well, then, we're as right as rain. We've only got to keep on going north-west – cross that little river, the what-do-you-call-it? – the Rush –"

"I know," said Peter. "The one that joins the big river at the Fords of Beruna, or Beruna's Bridge, as the D.L.F. calls it."

"That's right. Cross it and strike uphill, and we'll be at the Stone Table (Aslan's How, I mean) by eight or nine o'clock. I hope King Caspian will give us a good breakfast!"

"I hope you're right," said Susan. "I can't remember all that at all."

"That's the worst of girls," said Edmund to Peter and the Dwarf. "They never carry a map in their heads."

"That's because our heads have something inside them," said Lucy.

At first things seemed to be going pretty well. They

even thought they had struck an old path; but if you know anything about woods, you will know that one is always finding imaginary paths. They disappear after about five minutes and then you think you have found another (and hope it is not another but more of the same one) and it also disappears, and after you have been well lured out of your right direction you realize that none of them were paths at all. The boys and the Dwarf, however, were used to woods and were not taken in for more than a few seconds.

They had plodded on for about half an hour (three of them very stiff from yesterday's rowing) when Trumpkin suddenly whispered, "Stop." They all stopped. "There's something following us," he said in a low voice. "Or rather, something keeping up with us: over there on the left." They all stood still, listening and staring till their ears and eyes ached. "You and I'd better each have an arrow on the string," said Susan to Trumpkin. The Dwarf nodded, and when both bows were ready for action the party went on again.

They went a few dozen yards through fairly open woodland, keeping a sharp look-out. Then they came to a place where the undergrowth thickened and they had to pass nearer to it. Just as they were passing the place, there came a sudden something that snarled and flashed, rising out from the breaking twigs like a thunderbolt. Lucy was knocked down and winded, hearing the twang of a bowstring as she fell. When she was able to take notice of things again, she saw a great grim-looking grey bear lying dead with Trumpkin's arrow in its side.

"The D.L.F. beat you in *that* shooting match, Su," said

Peter, with a slightly forced smile. Even he had been shaken by this adventure.

"I – I left it too late," said Susan, in an embarrassed voice. "I was so afraid it might be, you know – one of our kind of bears, a *talking* bear." She hated killing things.

"That's the trouble of it," said Trumpkin, "when most of the beasts have gone enemy and gone dumb, but there are still some of the other kind left. You never know, and you daren't wait to see."

"Poor old Bruin," said Susan. "You don't think he *was*?"

"Not he," said the Dwarf. "I saw the face and I heard the snarl. He only wanted Little Girl for his breakfast. And talking of breakfast, I didn't want to discourage your Majesties when you said you hoped King Caspian would give you a good one: but meat's precious scarce in camp. And there's good eating on a bear. It would be a shame to leave the carcass without taking a bit, and it won't delay us more than half an hour. I dare say you two youngsters – Kings, I should say – know how to skin a bear?"

"Let's go and sit down a fair way off," said Susan to Lucy. "I know what a horrid messy business *that* will be." Lucy shuddered and nodded. When they had sat down she said: "Such a horrible idea has come into my head, Su."

"What's that?"

"Wouldn't it be dreadful if some day, in our own world, at home, men started going wild inside, like the animals here, and still looked like men, so that you'd never know which were which?"

"We've got enough to bother about here and now in

Narnia," said the practical Susan, "without imagining things like that."

When they rejoined the boys and the Dwarf, as much as they thought they could carry of the best meat had been cut off. Raw meat is not a nice thing to fill one's pockets with, but they folded it up in fresh leaves and made the best of it. They were all experienced enough to know that they would feel quite differently about these squashy and unpleasant parcels when they had walked long enough to be really hungry.

On they trudged again (stopping to wash three pairs of hands that needed it in the first stream they passed) until the sun rose and the birds began to sing, and more flies than they wanted were buzzing in the bracken. The stiffness from yesterday's rowing began to wear off. Everybody's spirits rose. The sun grew warmer and they took their helmets off and carried them.

"I suppose we *are* going right?" said Edmund about an hour later.

"I don't see how we can go wrong as long as we don't bear too much to the left," said Peter. "If we bear too much to the right, the worst that can happen is wasting a little time by striking the great River too soon and not cutting off the corner."

And again they trudged on with no sound except the thud of their feet and the jingle of their chain shirts.

"Where's this bally Rush got to?" said Edmund a good deal later.

"I certainly thought we'd have struck it by now," said Peter. "But there's nothing to do but keep on." They both knew that the Dwarf was looking anxiously at them, but he said nothing.

And still they trudged on and their mail shirts began to feel very hot and heavy.

"What on earth?" said Peter suddenly.

They had come, without seeing it, almost to the edge of a small precipice from which they looked down into a gorge with a river at the bottom. On the far side the cliffs rose much higher. None of the party except Edmund (and perhaps Trumpkin) was a rock climber.

"I'm sorry," said Peter. "It's my fault for coming this way. We're lost. I've never seen this place in my life before."

The Dwarf gave a low whistle between his teeth.

"Oh, do let's go back and go the other way," said Susan. "I knew all along we'd get lost in these woods."

"Susan!" said Lucy, reproachfully, "don't nag at Peter like that. It's so rotten, and he's doing all he can."

"And don't you snap at Su like that, either," said Edmund. "I think she's quite right."

"Tubs and tortoiseshells!" exclaimed Trumpkin. "If we've got lost coming, what chance have we of finding our way back? And if we're to go back to the Island and begin all over again – even supposing we could – we might as well give the whole thing up. Miraz will have finished with Caspian before we get there at that rate."

"You think we ought to go on?" said Lucy.

"I'm not sure the High King *is* lost," said Trumpkin. "What's to hinder this river being the Rush?"

"Because the Rush is not in a gorge," said Peter, keeping his temper with some difficulty.

"Your Majesty says *is*," replied the Dwarf, "but oughtn't you to say *was*? You knew this country hundreds – it may be a thousand – years ago. Mayn't it have changed? A landslide might have pulled off half the side of that hill, leaving bare rock, and there are your precipices beyond the gorge. Then the Rush might go on deepening its course year after year till you get the little precipices this side. Or there might have been an earthquake, or anything."

"I never thought of that," said Peter.

"And anyway," continued Trumpkin, "even if this is not the Rush, it's flowing roughly north and so it must

fall into the Great River anyway. I think I passed something that might have been it, on my way down. So if we go downstream, to our right, we'll hit the Great River. Perhaps not so high as we'd hoped, but at least we'll be no worse off than if you'd come my way."

"Trumpkin, you're a brick," said Peter. "Come on, then. Down this side of the gorge."

"Look! Look! Look!" cried Lucy.

"Where? What?" said everyone.

"The Lion," said Lucy. "Aslan himself. Didn't you

see?" Her face had changed completely and her eyes shone.

"Do you really mean –?" began Peter.

"Where did you think you saw him?" asked Susan.

"Don't talk like a grown-up," said Lucy, stamping her foot. "I didn't *think* I saw him. I saw him."

"Where, Lu?" asked Peter.

"Right up there between those mountain ashes. No, this side of the gorge. And up, not down. Just the opposite of the way you want to go. And he wanted us to go where he was – up there."

"How do you know that was what he wanted?" asked Edmund.

"He – I – I just know," said Lucy, "by his face."

The others all looked at each other in puzzled silence.

"Her Majesty may well have seen a lion," put in Trumpkin. "There are lions in these woods, I've been told. But it needn't have been a friendly and talking lion any more than the bear was a friendly and talking bear."

"Oh, don't be so stupid," said Lucy. "Do you think I don't know Aslan when I see him?"

"He'd be a pretty elderly lion by now," said Trumpkin, "if he's one you knew when you were here before! And if it could be the same one, what's to prevent him having gone wild and witless like so many others?"

Lucy turned crimson and I think she would have flown at Trumpkin, if Peter had not laid his hand on her arm. "The D.L.F. doesn't understand. How could he? You must just take it, Trumpkin, that we do really know about Aslan; a little bit about him, I mean. And you mustn't talk about him like that again. It isn't lucky for one thing: and it's all nonsense for another. The only question is whether Aslan was really there."

"But I know he was," said Lucy, her eyes filling with tears.

"Yes, Lu, but we don't, you see," said Peter.

"There's nothing for it but a vote," said Edmund.

"All right," replied Peter. "You're the eldest, D.L.F. What do you vote for? Up or down?"

"Down," said the Dwarf. "I know nothing about Aslan. But I do know that if we turn left and follow the gorge up, it might lead us all day before we found a place where we could cross it. Whereas if we turn right and go down, we're bound to reach the Great River in about a couple of hours. And if there *are* any real lions about, we want to go away from them, not towards them."

"What do you say, Susan?"

"Don't be angry, Lu," said Susan, "but I do think we should go down. I'm dead tired. Do let's get out of this wretched wood into the open as quick as we can. And none of us except you saw *anything*."

"Edmund?" said Peter.

"Well, there's just this," said Edmund, speaking quickly and turning a little red. "When we first discovered Narnia a year ago – or a thousand years ago, whichever it is – it was Lucy who discovered it first and none of us would believe her. I was the worst of the lot, I know. Yet she was right after all. Wouldn't it be fair to believe her this time? I vote for going up."

"Oh, Ed!" said Lucy and seized his hand.

"And now it's your turn, Peter," said Susan, "and I do hope –"

"Oh, shut up, shut up and let a chap think,"

interrupted Peter. "I'd much rather not have to vote."

"You're the High King," said Trumpkin sternly.

"Down," said Peter after a long pause. "I know Lucy may be right after all, but I can't help it. We must do one or the other."

So they set off to their right along the edge, downstream. And Lucy came last of the party, crying bitterly.

CHAPTER TEN

THE RETURN OF THE LION

To keep along the edge of the gorge was not so easy as it had looked. Before they had gone many yards they were confronted with young fir woods growing on the very edge, and after they had tried to go through these, stooping and pushing for about ten minutes, they realized that, in there, it would take them an hour to do half a mile. So they came back and out again and decided to go round the fir wood. This took them much farther to their right than they wanted to go, far out of sight of the cliffs and out of sound of the river, till they began to be afraid they had lost it altogether. Nobody knew the time, but it was getting to the hottest part of the day.

When they were able at last to go back to the edge of the gorge (nearly a mile below the point from which they had started) they found the cliffs on their side of it a good deal lower and more broken. Soon they found a way down into the gorge and continued the journey at the river's edge. But first they had a rest and a long drink. No one was talking any more about breakfast, or even dinner, with Caspian.

They may have been wise to stick to the Rush instead of going along the top. It kept them sure of their direction: and ever since the fir wood they had all been afraid of being forced too far out of their course and losing themselves in the wood. It was an old and pathless forest, and you could not keep anything like a straight course in it. Patches of hopeless brambles, fallen trees, boggy places and dense undergrowth would be always getting in your way. But the gorge of the Rush was not at all a nice place for travelling either. I mean, it was not a nice place for people in a hurry. For an afternoon's ramble ending in a picnic tea it would have been delightful. It had everything you could want on an occasion of that sort – rumbling waterfalls, silver cascades, deep, amber-coloured pools, mossy rocks, and deep moss on the banks in which you could sink over your ankles, every kind of fern, jewel-like dragon flies, sometimes a hawk overhead and once (Peter and Trumpkin both thought) an eagle. But of course what

the children and the Dwarf wanted to see as soon as possible was the Great River below them, and Beruna, and the way to Aslan's How.

As they went on, the Rush began to fall more and more steeply. Their journey became more and more of a climb and less and less of a walk – in places even a dangerous climb over slippery rock with a nasty drop into dark chasms, and the river roaring angrily at the bottom.

You may be sure they watched the cliffs on their left eagerly for any sign of a break or any place where they could climb them; but those cliffs remained cruel. It was maddening, because everyone knew that if once they were out of the gorge on that side, they would have only a smooth slope and a fairly short walk to Caspian's headquarters.

The boys and the Dwarf were now in favour of lighting a fire and cooking their bear-meat. Susan didn't want this; she only wanted, as she said, "to get *on* and finish it and get out of these beastly woods". Lucy was far too tired and miserable to have any opinion about anything. But as there was no dry wood to be had, it mattered very little what anyone thought. The boys began to wonder if raw meat was really as nasty as they had always been told. Trumpkin assured them it was.

Of course, if the children had attempted a journey like this a few days ago in England, they would have been knocked up. I think I have explained before how Narnia was altering them. Even Lucy was by now, so to speak, only one-third of a little girl going to boarding school for the first time, and two-thirds of Queen Lucy of Narnia.

"At last!" said Susan.

"Oh, hurray!" said Peter.

The river gorge had just made a bend and the whole view spread out beneath them. They could see open country stretching before them to the horizon and, between it and them, the broad silver

ribbon of the Great River. They could see the specially broad and shallow place which had once been the Fords of Beruna but was now spanned by a long, many-arched bridge. There was a little town at the far end of it.

"By Jove," said Edmund. "We fought the Battle of Beruna just where that town is!"

This cheered the boys more than anything. You can't help feeling stronger when you look at a place where you won a glorious victory not to mention a kingdom, hundreds of years ago. Peter and Edmund were soon so busy talking about the battle that they forgot their sore feet and the heavy drag of their mail shirts on their shoulders. The Dwarf was interested too.

They were all getting on at a quicker pace now. The going became easier. Though there were still sheer cliffs on their left, the ground was becoming lower on their right. Soon it was no longer a gorge at all, only a valley. There were no more waterfalls and presently they were in fairly thick woods again.

Then – all at once – *whizz*, and a sound rather like the stroke of a woodpecker. The children were still wondering where (ages ago) they had heard a sound just like that and why they disliked it so, when Trumpkin shouted, "Down', at the same moment forcing Lucy (who happened to be next to him) flat down into the bracken. Peter, who had been looking up to see if he could spot a squirrel, had seen what it was – a long cruel arrow had sunk into a tree trunk just above his head. As he pulled Susan down and dropped himself, another came rasping over his shoulder and struck the ground at his side.

"Quick! Quick! Get back! *Crawl*!" panted Trumpkin.

They turned and wriggled along uphill, under the

bracken amid clouds of horribly buzzing flies. Arrows whizzed round them. One struck Susan's helmet with a sharp ping and glanced off. They crawled quicker. Sweat poured off them. Then they ran, stooping nearly double. The boys held their swords in their hands for fear they would trip them up.

It was heart-breaking work – all uphill again, back over the ground they had already travelled. When they felt that they really couldn't run any more, even to save their lives,

they all dropped down in the damp moss beside a waterfall and behind a big boulder, panting. They were surprised to see how high they had already got.

They listened intently and heard no sound of pursuit.

"So *that's* all right," said Trumpkin, drawing a deep breath. "They're not searching the wood. Only sentries, I expect. But it means that Miraz has an outpost down there. Bottles and battledores! though, it was a near thing."

"I ought to have my head smacked for bringing us this way at all," said Peter.

"On the contrary, your Majesty," said the Dwarf. "For one thing it wasn't you, it was your royal brother, King Edmund, who first suggested going by Glasswater."

"I'm afraid the D.L.F.'s right," said Edmund, who had quite honestly forgotten this ever since things began going wrong.

"And for another," continued Trumpkin, "if we'd gone my way, we'd have walked straight into that new outpost, most likely; or at least had just the same trouble avoiding it. I think this Glasswater route has turned out for the best."

"A blessing in disguise," said Susan.

"Some disguise!" said Edmund.

"I suppose we'll have to go right up the gorge again now," said Lucy.

"Lu, you're a hero," said Peter. "That's the nearest you've got today to saying *I told you so*. Let's get on."

"And as soon as we're well up into the forest," said Trumpkin, "whatever anyone says, I'm going to light a fire and cook supper. But we must get well away from here."

There is no need to describe how they toiled back up the gorge. It was pretty hard work, but oddly enough everyone felt more cheerful. They were getting their second wind; and the word *supper* had had a wonderful effect.

They reached the fir wood which had caused them so much trouble while it was still daylight, and bivouacked in a hollow just above it. It was tedious gathering the firewood; but it was grand when the fire blazed up and they began producing the damp and smeary parcels of bear-meat which would have been so very unattractive to anyone who had spent the day indoors. The Dwarf had splendid ideas about cookery. Each apple (they still had a few of these) was wrapped up in bear's meat – as if it was to be apple dumpling with meat instead of pastry, only much thicker – and spiked on a sharp stick and then roasted. And the juice of the apple worked all through the meat, like apple sauce with roast pork. Bear that has lived too much on other animals is not very nice, but bear that has had plenty of honey and fruit is excellent, and this turned out to be that sort of bear. It was a truly glorious meal. And, of course, no washing up – only lying back and watching the smoke from Trumpkin's pipe and stretching one's tired legs and chatting. Everyone felt quite hopeful now about finding King Caspian tomorrow and defeating Miraz in a few days. It may not have been sensible of them to feel like this, but they did.

They dropped off to sleep one by one, but all pretty quickly.

Lucy woke out of the deepest sleep you can imagine, with the feeling that the voice she liked best in the world had been calling her name. She thought at first it was her father's voice, but that did not seem quite right. Then she thought it was Peter's voice, but that did not seem to fit either. She did not want to get up; not because she was still tired – on the contrary she was wonderfully rested and all the aches had gone from her bones – but because she felt so extremely happy and comfortable. She was looking straight up at the Narnian moon, which is larger than ours, and at the starry sky, for the place where they had bivouacked was comparatively open.

"Lucy," came the call again, neither her father's voice nor Peter's. She sat up, trembling with excitement but not with fear. The moon was so bright that the whole forest landscape around her was almost as clear as day, though it looked wilder. Behind her was the fir wood; away to her right the jagged cliff-tops on the far side of the gorge; straight ahead, open grass to where a glade of trees began about a bow-shot away. Lucy looked very hard at the trees of that glade.

"Why, I do believe they're moving," she said to herself. "They're walking about."

She got up, her heart beating wildly, and walked towards them. There was certainly a noise in the glade, a noise such as trees make in a high wind, though there was no wind tonight. Yet it was not exactly an ordinary tree-noise either. Lucy felt there was a tune in it, but she could not catch the tune any more than she had been able to catch the words when the trees had so nearly talked to her the night before. But there was, at least, a lilt; she felt her own feet wanting to dance as she got nearer. And now there was no doubt that the trees were really moving – moving in and out through one another as if in a complicated country dance. ("And I suppose," thought Lucy, "when trees dance, it must be a very, very country dance indeed.') She was almost among them now.

The first tree she looked at seemed at first glance to be not a tree at all but a huge man with a shaggy beard and great bushes of hair. She was not frightened: she had seen such things before. But when she looked again he was only a tree, though he was still moving. You couldn't see whether he had feet or roots, of course, because when trees move they don't walk on the surface of the earth; they wade in it as we do in water. The same thing happened with every tree she looked at. At one moment they seemed to be the friendly, lovely giant and giantess forms which the tree-people put on when some good magic has called them into full life: next moment they all looked like trees again. But when they looked like trees, it was like strangely human trees, and when they looked like people, it was like strangely branchy and leafy people – and all the time that queer lilting, rustling, cool, merry noise.

"They are almost awake, not quite," said Lucy. She knew she herself was wide awake, wider than anyone usually is.

She went fearlessly in among them, dancing herself as she leaped this way and that to avoid being run into by these huge partners. But she was only half interested in them. She wanted to get beyond them to something else; it was from beyond them that the dear voice had called.

She soon got through them (half wondering whether she had been using her arms to push branches aside, or to take hands in a Great Chain with big dancers who stooped to reach her) for they were really a ring of trees round a central open place. She stepped out from among their shifting confusion of lovely lights and shadows.

A circle of grass, smooth as a lawn, met her eyes, with dark trees dancing all round it. And then – oh joy! For *he* was there: the huge Lion, shining white in the moonlight, with his huge black shadow underneath him.

But for the movement of his tail he might have been a stone lion, but Lucy never thought of that. She never stopped to think whether he was a friendly lion or not. She rushed to him. She felt her heart would burst if she lost a moment. And the next thing she knew was that she was kissing him and putting her arms as far round his neck as

she could and burying her face in the beautiful rich silkiness of his mane.

"Aslan, Aslan. Dear Aslan," sobbed Lucy. "At last."

The great beast rolled over on his side so that Lucy fell, half sitting and half lying between his front paws. He bent forward and just touched her nose with his tongue. His warm breath came all round her. She gazed up into the large wise face.

"Welcome, child," he said.

"Aslan," said Lucy, "you're bigger."

"That is because you are older, little one," answered he.

"Not because you are?"

"I am not. But every year you grow, you will find me bigger."

For a time she was so happy that she did not want to speak. But Aslan spoke.

"Lucy," he said, "we must not lie here for long. You have work in hand, and much time has been lost today."

"Yes, wasn't it a shame?" said Lucy. "*I* saw you all right. They wouldn't believe me. They're all so –"

From somewhere deep inside Aslan's body there came the faintest suggestion of a growl.

"I'm sorry," said Lucy, who understood some of his moods. "I didn't mean to start slanging the others. But it wasn't my fault anyway, was it?"

The Lion looked straight into her eyes.

"Oh, Aslan," said Lucy. "You don't mean it was? How could I – I couldn't have left the others and come up to you alone, how could I? Don't look at me like that . . . oh well, I suppose I *could*. Yes, and it wouldn't have been alone, I know, not if I was with you. But what would have been the good?"

Aslan said nothing.

"You mean," said Lucy rather faintly, "that it would have turned out all right – somehow? But how? Please, Aslan! Am I not to know?"

"To know what *would* have happened, child?" said Aslan. "No. Nobody is ever told that."

"Oh dear," said Lucy.

"But anyone can find out what *will* happen," said Aslan. "If you go back to the others now, and wake them up; and tell them you have seen me again; and that you must all get up at once and follow me – what will happen? There is only one way of finding out."

"Do you mean that is what you want me to do?" gasped Lucy.

"Yes, little one," said Aslan.

"Will the others see you too?" asked Lucy.

"Certainly not at first," said Aslan. "Later on, it depends."

"But they won't believe me!" said Lucy.

"It doesn't matter," said Aslan.

"Oh dear, oh dear," said Lucy. "And I was so pleased at finding you again. And I thought you'd let me stay. And I thought you'd come roaring in and frighten all the enemies away – like last time. And now everything is going to be horrid."

"It is hard for you, little one," said Aslan. "But things never happen the same way twice. It has been hard for us all in Narnia before now."

Lucy buried her head in his mane to hide from his face. But there must have been magic in his mane. She could feel lion-strength going into her. Quite suddenly she sat up.

"I'm sorry, Aslan," she said. "I'm ready now."

"Now you are a lioness," said Aslan. "And now all Narnia will be renewed. But come. We have no time to lose."

He got up and walked with stately, noiseless paces back to the belt of dancing trees through which she had just come: and Lucy went with him, laying a rather tremulous hand on his mane. The trees parted to let them through and for one second assumed their human forms completely. Lucy had a glimpse of tall and lovely wood-gods and wood-goddesses all bowing to the Lion; next moment they were trees again, but still bowing, with such graceful sweeps of branch and trunk that their bowing was itself a kind of dance.

"Now, child," said Aslan, when they had left the trees behind them, "I will wait here. Go and wake the others and tell them to follow. If they will not, then you at least must follow me alone."

It is a terrible thing to have to wake four people, all older than yourself and all very tired, for the purpose of telling them something they probably won't believe and making them do something they certainly won't like. "I mustn't think about it, I must just do it," thought Lucy.

She went to Peter first and shook him. "Peter," she whispered in his ear, "wake up. Quick. Aslan is here. He says we've got to follow him at once."

"Certainly, Lu. Whatever you like," said Peter unexpectedly. This was encouraging, but as Peter instantly rolled round and went to sleep again it wasn't much use.

Then she tried Susan. Susan did really wake up, but only to say in her most annoying grown-up voice, "You've been dreaming, Lucy. Go to sleep again."

She tackled Edmund next. It was very difficult to wake

him, but when at last she had done it he was really awake and sat up.

"Eh?" he said in a grumpy voice. "What are you talking about?"

She said it all over again. This was one of the worst parts of her job, for each time she said it, it sounded less convincing.

"Aslan!" said Edmund, jumping up. "Hurray! Where?"

Lucy turned back to where she could see the Lion waiting, his patient eyes fixed upon her. "There," she said, pointing.

"Where?" asked Edmund again.

"There. There. Don't you see? Just this side of the trees."

Edmund stared hard for a while and then said, "No. There's nothing there. You've got dazzled and muddled with the moonlight. One does, you know. I thought I saw something for a moment myself. It's only an optical what-do-you-call-it."

"I can see him all the time," said Lucy. "He's looking straight at us."

"Then why can't I see him?"

"He said you mightn't be able to."

"Why?"

"I don't know. That's what he said."

"Oh, bother it all," said Edmund. "I do wish you wouldn't keep on seeing things. But I suppose we'll have to wake the others."

CHAPTER ELEVEN

THE LION ROARS

When the whole party was finally awake Lucy had to tell her story for the fourth time. The blank silence which followed it was as discouraging as anything could be.

"I can't see anything," said Peter after he had stared his eyes sore. "Can you, Susan?"

"No, of course I can't," snapped Susan. "Because there isn't anything to see. She's been dreaming. Do lie down and go to sleep, Lucy."

"And I do hope," said Lucy in a tremulous voice, "that you will all come with me. Because – because I'll have to go with him whether anyone else does or not."

"Don't talk nonsense, Lucy," said Susan. "Of course you can't go off on your own. Don't let her, Peter. She's being downright naughty."

"I'll go with her, if she *must* go," said Edmund. "She's been right before."

"I know she has," said Peter. "And she may have been right this morning. We certainly had no luck going down the gorge. Still – at this hour of the night. And why should Aslan be invisible to us? He never used to be. It's not like him. What does the D.L.F. say?"

"Oh, I say nothing at all," answered the Dwarf. "If you all go, of course, I'll go with you; and if your party splits up, I'll go with the High King. That's my duty to him and King Caspian. But, if you ask my private opinion, I'm a plain dwarf who doesn't think there's much chance of finding a road by night where you couldn't find one by day. And I have no use for magic lions which are talking lions and don't talk, and friendly lions though they don't do us any good, and whopping big lions though nobody can see them. It's all bilge and beanstalks as far as I can see."

"He's beating his paw on the ground for us to hurry," said Lucy. "We must go *now*. At least I must."

"You've no right to try to force the rest of us like that. It's four to one and you're the youngest," said Susan.

"Oh, come on," growled Edmund. "We've got to go. There'll be no peace till we do." He fully intended to back Lucy up, but he was annoyed at losing his night's sleep and was making up for it by doing everything as sulkily as possible.

"On the march, then," said Peter, wearily fitting his arm into his shield-strap and putting his helmet on. At any other time he would have said something nice to Lucy, who was his favourite sister, for he knew how wretched she must be feeling, and he knew that, whatever had happened, it was not her fault. But he couldn't help being a little annoyed with her all the same.

Susan was the worst. "Supposing *I* started behaving like Lucy," she said. "I might threaten to stay here whether the rest of you went on or not. I jolly well think I shall."

"Obey the High King, your Majesty," said Trumpkin, "and let's be off. If I'm not to be allowed to sleep, I'd as soon march as stand here talking."

And so at last they got on the move. Lucy went first, biting her lip and trying not to say all the things she thought of saying to Susan. But she forgot them when she fixed her eyes on Aslan. He turned and walked at a slow pace about thirty yards ahead of them. The others had only Lucy's directions to guide them, for Aslan was not only invisible to them but silent as well. His big cat-like paws made no noise on the grass.

He led them to the right of the dancing trees – whether they were still dancing nobody knew, for Lucy had her eyes on the Lion and the rest had their eyes on Lucy – and nearer the edge of the gorge. "Cobbles and kettledrums!" thought Trumpkin. "I hope this madness isn't going to end in a moonlight climb and broken necks."

For a long way Aslan went along the top of the precipices. Then they came to a place where some little trees grew right on the edge. He turned and disappeared among them. Lucy held her breath, for it looked as if he had plunged over the cliff; but she was too busy keeping him in sight to stop and think about this. She quickened her pace and was soon among the trees herself. Looking down, she could see a steep and narrow path going slantwise down into the gorge between rocks, and Aslan descending it. He turned and looked at her with his happy eyes. Lucy clapped her hands and began to scramble down after him. From behind her she heard the voices of the others shouting, "Hi! Lucy! Look out, for goodness' sake. You're right on the edge of the gorge. Come back – " and then, a moment later, Edmund's voice saying, "No, she's right. There *is* a way down."

Half-way down the path Edmund caught up with her.

"Look!" he said in great excitement. "Look! What's that shadow crawling down in front of us?"

"It's *his* shadow," said Lucy.

"I do believe you're right, Lu," said Edmund. "I can't think how I didn't see it before. But where is he?"

"With his shadow, of course. Can't you see him?"

"Well, I almost thought I did – for a moment. It's such a rum light."

"Get on, King Edmund, get on," came Trumpkin's voice from behind and above: and then, farther behind and still nearly at the top, Peter's voice saying, "Oh, buck up, Susan. Give me your hand. Why, a baby could get down here. And do stop grousing."

In a few minutes they were at the bottom and the roaring of water filled their ears. Treading delicately, like a cat, Aslan stepped from stone to stone across the stream. In the middle he stopped, bent down to drink, and as he raised his shaggy head, dripping from the water, he turned to face them again. This time Edmund saw him. "Oh, Aslan!" he cried, darting forward. But the Lion whisked round and began padding up the slope on the far side of the Rush.

"Peter, Peter," cried Edmund. "Did you see?"

"I saw something," said Peter. "But it's so tricky in this moonlight. On we go, though, and three cheers for Lucy. I don't feel half so tired now, either."

Aslan without hesitation led them to their left, farther up the gorge. The whole journey was odd and dream-like – the roaring stream, the wet grey grass, the glimmering cliffs which they were approaching, and always the glorious, silently pacing Beast ahead. Everyone except Susan and the Dwarf could see him now.

Presently they came to another steep path, up the face of the farther precipices. These were far higher than the ones they had just descended, and the journey up them was a long and tedious zig-zag. Fortunately the Moon shone right above the gorge so that neither side was in shadow.

Lucy was nearly blown when the tail and hind legs of Aslan disappeared over the top: but with one last effort she scrambled after him and came out, rather shaky-legged and breathless, on the hill they had been trying to reach ever since they left Glasswater. The long gentle slope (heather and grass and a few very big rocks that shone white in the moonlight) stretched up to where it vanished in a glimmer of trees about half a mile away. She knew it. It was the hill of the Stone Table.

With a jingling of mail the others climbed up behind her. Aslan glided on before them and they walked after him.

"Lucy," said Susan in a very small voice.

"Yes?" said Lucy.

"I see him now. I'm sorry."

"That's all right."

"But I've been far worse than you know. I really believed it was him – he, I mean – yesterday. When he warned us not to go down to the fir wood. And I really believed it was him tonight, when you woke us up. I mean, deep down inside. Or I could have, if I'd let myself. But I just wanted to get out of the woods and – and – oh, I don't know. And what ever am I to say to him?"

"Perhaps you won't need to say much," suggested Lucy.

Soon they reached the trees and through them the children could see the Great Mound, Aslan's How, which had been raised over the Table since their days.

"Our side don't keep very good watch," muttered Trumpkin. "We ought to have been challenged before now –"

"Hush!" said the other four, for now Aslan had stopped and turned and stood facing them, looking so majestic that they felt as glad as anyone can who feels afraid, and as afraid as anyone can who feels glad. The boys strode forward: Lucy made way for them: Susan and the Dwarf shrank back.

"Oh, Aslan," said King Peter, dropping on one knee and raising the Lion's heavy paw to his face, "I'm so glad. And I'm so sorry. I've been leading them wrong ever since we started and especially yesterday morning."

"My dear son," said Aslan.

Then he turned and welcomed Edmund. "Well done," were his words.

Then, after an awful pause, the deep voice said, "Susan." Susan made no answer but the others thought she was crying. "You have listened to fears, child," said Aslan. "Come, let me breathe on you. Forget them. Are you brave again?"

"A little, Aslan," said Susan.

"And now!" said Aslan in a much louder voice with just a hint of roar in it, while his tail lashed his flanks. "And now, where is this little Dwarf, this famous swordsman and archer, who doesn't believe in lions? Come here, son of Earth, come HERE!" – and the last word was no longer the hint of a roar but almost the real thing.

"Wraiths and wreckage!" gasped Trumpkin in the ghost of a voice. The children, who knew Aslan well enough to see that he liked the Dwarf very much, were not disturbed; but it was quite another thing for Trumpkin, who had never seen a lion before, let alone this Lion. He did the only sensible thing he could have done; that is, instead of bolting, he tottered towards Aslan.

Aslan pounced. Have you ever seen a very young kitten being carried in the mother cat's mouth? It was like that. The Dwarf, hunched up in a little, miserable ball, hung from Aslan's mouth. The Lion gave him one shake and all his armour rattled like a tinker's pack and then – hey-presto – the Dwarf flew up in the air. He was as safe as if he had been in bed, though he did not feel so. As he came down the huge velvety paws caught him as gently as a

mother's arms and set him (right way up, too) on the ground.

"Son of Earth, shall we be friends?" asked Aslan.

"Ye – he – he – hes," panted the Dwarf, for it had not yet got its breath back.

"Now," said Aslan. "The Moon is setting. Look behind you: there is the dawn beginning. We have no time to lose. You three, you sons of Adam and son of Earth, hasten into the Mound and deal with what you will find there."

The Dwarf was still speechless and neither of the boys dared to ask if Aslan would follow them. All three drew their swords and saluted, then turned and jingled away into the dusk. Lucy noticed that there was no sign of weariness in their faces: both the High King and King Edmund looked more like men than boys.

The girls watched them out of sight, standing close beside Aslan. The light was changing. Low down in the east, Aravir, the morning star of Narnia, gleamed like a little moon. Aslan, who seemed larger than before, lifted his head, shook his mane, and roared.

The sound, deep and throbbing at first like an organ beginning on a low note, rose and became louder, and then far louder again, till the earth and air were shaking with it. It rose up from that hill and floated across all Narnia. Down in Miraz's camp men woke, stared palely in one another's faces, and grasped their weapons. Down below that in the Great River, now at its coldest hour, the heads and shoulders of the nymphs, and the great weedy-bearded head of the river-god, rose from the water. Beyond it, in every field and wood, the alert ears of rabbits rose from their holes, the sleepy heads of birds came out from under wings, owls hooted, vixens barked, hedgehogs grunted, the trees stirred. In towns and villages mothers pressed babies close to their breasts, staring with wild eyes, dogs whimpered, and men leaped up groping for lights. Far away on the northern frontier the mountain giants peered from the dark gateways of their castles.

What Lucy and Susan saw was a dark something coming to them from almost every direction across the hills. It looked first like a black mist creeping on the ground, then

like the stormy waves of a black sea rising higher and higher as it came on, and then, at last, like what it was – woods on the move. All the trees of the world appeared to be rushing towards Aslan. But as they drew nearer they looked less like trees, and when the whole crowd, bowing and curtsying and waving thin long arms to Aslan, were all around Lucy, she saw that it was a crowd of human shapes. Pale birch-girls were tossing their heads, willow-women pushed back their hair from their brooding faces to gaze on Aslan, the queenly beeches stood still and adored

him, shaggy oak-men, lean and melancholy elms, shock-headed hollies (dark themselves, but their wives all bright with berries) and gay rowans, all bowed and rose again, shouting, "Aslan, Aslan!" in their various husky or creaking or wave-like voices.

The crowd and the dance round Aslan (for it had become a dance once more) grew so thick and rapid that Lucy was confused. She never saw where certain other people came from who were soon capering about among the trees. One was a youth, dressed only in a fawn-skin, with vine-leaves wreathed in his curly hair. His face would have been almost too pretty for a boy's, if it had not looked so extremely wild. You felt, as Edmund said when he saw him a few days later, "There's a chap who might do anything – absolutely anything." He seemed to have a great many names – Bromios, Bassareus, and the Ram were three of them. There were a lot of girls with him, as wild as he. There was even, unexpectedly, someone on a donkey. And everybody was laughing: and everybody was shouting out, "Euan, euan, eu-oi-oi-oi."

"Is it a Romp, Aslan?" cried the youth. And apparently it was. But nearly everyone seemed to have a different idea as to what they were playing. It may have been Tig, but Lucy never discovered who was It. It was rather like Blind Man's Buff, only everyone behaved as if they were blindfolded. It was not unlike Hunt the Slipper, but the slipper was never found. What made it more complicated was that the man on the donkey, who was old and enormously fat, began calling out at once, "Refreshments! Time for refreshments," and falling off his donkey and being bundled on to it again by the others, while the donkey was under the impression that the whole thing was a circus and tried to give a display of walking on its hind legs. And all the time there were more and more vine leaves everywhere. And soon not only leaves but vines. They were climbing up everything. They were running up the legs of the tree people and circling round their necks. Lucy put up her hands to push back her hair and found she was pushing back vine branches. The donkey was a mass of them. His tail was completely entangled and something dark was nodding between his ears. Lucy looked again and saw it was a bunch of grapes. After that it was mostly grapes – overhead and underfoot and all around.

"Refreshments! Refreshments," roared the old man.

Everyone began eating, and whatever hothouses your people may have, you have never tasted such grapes. Really good grapes, firm and tight on the outside, but bursting into cool sweetness when you put them into your mouth, were one of the things the girls had never had quite enough of before. Here, there were more than anyone could possibly want, and no table-manners at all. One saw sticky and stained fingers everywhere, and, though mouths were full, the laughter never ceased nor the yodelling cries of *Euan, euan, eu-oi-oi-oi-oi*, till all of a sudden everyone felt at the same moment that the game (whatever it was), and the feast, ought to be over, and everyone flopped down breathless on the ground and turned their faces to Aslan to hear what he would say next.

At that moment the sun was just rising and Lucy remembered something and whispered to Susan,

"I say, Su, I know who they are."

"Who?"

"The boy with the wild face is Bacchus and the old one on the donkey is Silenus. Don't you remember Mr Tumnus telling us about them long ago?"

"Yes, of course. But I say, Lu –"

"What?"

"I wouldn't have felt safe with Bacchus and all his wild girls if we'd met them without Aslan."

"I should think not," said Lucy.

CHAPTER TWELVE

SORCERY AND SUDDEN VENGEANCE

MEANWHILE Trumpkin and the two boys arrived at the dark little stone archway which led into the inside of the Mound, and two sentinel badgers (the white patches on their cheeks were all Edmund could see of them) leaped up with bared teeth and asked them in snarling voices, "Who goes there?"

"Trumpkin," said the Dwarf. "Bringing the High King of Narnia out of the far past."

The badgers nosed at the boys' hands. "At last," they said. "At last."

"Give us a light, friends," said Trumpkin.

The badgers found a torch just inside the arch and Peter lit it and handed it to Trumpkin. "The D.L.F. had better lead," he said. "We don't know our way about this place."

Trumpkin took the torch and went ahead into the dark tunnel. It was a cold, black, musty place, with an occasional bat fluttering in the torchlight, and plenty of cobwebs. The boys, who had been mostly in the open air since that morning at the railway station, felt as if they were going into a trap or a prison.

"I say, Peter," whispered Edmund. "Look at those carvings on the walls. Don't they look old? And yet we're older than that. When we were last here, they hadn't been made."

"Yes," said Peter. "That makes one think."

The Dwarf went on ahead and then turned to the right, and then to the left, and then down some steps, and then to the left again. Then at last they saw a light ahead – light from under a door. And now for the first time they heard voices, for they had come to the door of the central chamber. The voices inside were angry ones. Someone was talking so loudly that the approach of the boys and the Dwarf had not been heard.

"Don't like the sound of that," whispered Trumpkin to Peter. "Let's listen for a moment." All three stood perfectly still on the outside of the door.

"You know well enough," said a voice ("That's the

King," whispered Trumpkin), "why the Horn was not blown at sunrise this morning. Have you forgotten that Miraz fell upon us almost before Trumpkin had gone, and we were fighting for our lives for the space of three hours and more? I blew it when first I had a breathing space."

"I'm not likely to forgot it," came the angry voice, "when my Dwarfs bore the brunt of the attack and one in five of them fell." ("That's Nikabrik," whispered Trumpkin.)

"For shame, Dwarf," came a thick voice ("Truffle-hunter's," said Trumpkin). "We all did as much as the Dwarfs and none more than the King."

"Tell that tale your own way for all I care," answered

Nikabrik. "But whether it was that the Horn was blown too late, or whether there was no magic in it, no help has come. You, you great clerk, you master magician, you know-all; are you still asking us to hang our hopes on Aslan and King Peter and all the rest of it?"

"I must confess – I cannot deny it – that I am deeply disappointed in the result of the operation," came the answer. ("That'll be Doctor Cornelius," said Trumpkin.)

"To speak plainly," said Nikabrik, "your wallet's empty, your eggs addled, your fish uncaught, your promises broken. Stand aside then and let others work. And that is why –"

"The help will come," said Trufflehunter. "I stand by Aslan. Have patience, like us beasts. The help will come. It may be even now at the door."

"Pah!" snarled Nikabrik. "You badgers would have us wait till the sky falls and we can all catch larks. I tell you we *can't* wait. Food is running short; we lose more than we can afford at every encounter; our followers are slipping away."

"And why?" asked Trufflehunter. "I'll tell you why. Because it is noised among them that we have called on the Kings of old and the Kings of old have not answered. The last words Trumpkin spoke before he went (and went, most likely, to his death) were, 'If you must blow the Horn, do not let the army know why you blow it or what you hope from it.' But that same evening everyone seemed to know."

"You'd better have shoved your grey snout in a hornets' nest, Badger, than suggest that I am the blab," said Nikabrik. "Take it back, or –"

"Oh, stop it, both of you," said King Caspian. "I want

to know what it is that Nikabrik keeps on hinting we should do. But before that, I want to know who those two strangers are whom he has brought into our council and who stand there with their ears open and their mouths shut."

"They are friends of mine," said Nikabrik. "And what better right have you yourself to be here than that you are a friend of Trumpkin's and the Badger's? And what right has that old dotard in the black gown to be here except that he is your friend? Why am I to be the only one who can't bring in his friends?"

"His Majesty is the King to whom you have sworn allegiance," said Trufflehunter sternly.

"Court manners, court manners," sneered Nikabrik. "But in this hole we may talk plainly. You know – and he knows – that this Telmarine boy will be king of nowhere and nobody in a week unless we can help him out of the trap in which he sits."

"Perhaps," said Cornelius, "your new friends would like to speak for themselves? You there, who and what are you?"

"Worshipful Master Doctor," came a thin, whining voice. "So please you, I'm only a poor old woman, I am, and very obliged to his Worshipful Dwarfship for his friendship, I'm sure. His Majesty, bless his handsome face, has no need to be afraid of an old woman that's nearly doubled up with the rheumatics and hasn't two sticks to put under her kettle. I have some poor little skill – not like yours, Master Doctor, of course – in small spells and cantrips that I'd be glad to use against our enemies if it was agreeable to all concerned. For I hate 'em. Oh yes. No one hates better than me."

"That is all most interesting and – er – satisfactory," said Doctor Cornelius. "I think I now know what you are, Madam. Perhaps your other friend, Nikabrik, would give some account of himself?"

A dull, grey voice at which Peter's flesh crept replied, "I'm hunger. I'm thirst. Where I bite, I hold till I die, and even after death they must cut out my mouthful from my enemy's body and bury it with me. I can fast a hundred years and not die. I can lie a hundred nights on the ice and not freeze. I can drink a river of blood and not burst. Show me your enemies."

"And it is in the presence of these two that you wish to disclose your plan?" said Caspian.

"Yes," said Nikabrik. "And by their help that I mean to execute it."

There was a minute or two during which Trumpkin and the boys could hear Caspian and his two friends speaking in low voices but could not make out what they were saying. Then Caspian spoke aloud.

"Well, Nikabrik," he said, "we will hear your plan."

There was a pause so long that the boys began to wonder if Nikabrik was ever going to begin; when he did, it was in a lower voice, as if he himself did not much like what he was saying.

"All said and done," he muttered, "none of us knows the truth about the ancient days in Narnia. Trumpkin believed none of the stories. I was ready to put them to the trial. We tried first the Horn and it has failed. If there ever was a High King Peter and a Queen Susan and a King Edmund and a Queen Lucy, then either they have not heard us, or they cannot come, or they are our enemies –"

"Or they are on the way," put in Trufflehunter.

"You can go on saying that till Miraz has fed us all to his dogs. As I was saying, we have tried one link in the chain of old legends, and it has done us no good. Well. But when your sword breaks, you draw your dagger. The stories tell of other powers beside the ancient Kings and Queens. How if we could call *them* up?"

"If you mean Aslan," said Trufflehunter, "it's all one calling on him and on the Kings. They were his servants. If he will not send them (but I make no doubt he will), is he more likely to come himself?"

"No. You're right there," said Nikabrik. "Aslan and the Kings go together. Either Aslan is dead, or he is not on our side. Or else something stronger than himself keeps him back. And if he did come – how do we know he'd be our friend? He was not always a good friend to Dwarfs by all that's told. Not even to all beasts. Ask the Wolves. And anyway, he was in Narnia only once that I ever heard of, and he didn't stay long. You may drop Aslan out of the reckoning. I was thinking of someone else."

There was no answer, and for a few minutes it was so still that Edmund could hear the wheezy and snuffling breath of the Badger.

"Who do you mean?" said Caspian at last.

"I mean a power so much greater than Aslan's that it held Narnia spellbound for years and years, if the stories are true."

"The White Witch!" cried three voices all at once, and from the noise Peter guessed that three people had leaped to their feet.

"Yes," said Nikabrik very slowly and distinctly, "I mean the Witch. Sit down again. Don't all take fright at a name as if you were children. We want power: and we want a power that will be on our side. As for power, do not the stories say that the Witch defeated Aslan, and bound him, and killed him on that very stone which is over there, just beyond the light?"

"But they also say that he came to life again," said the Badger sharply.

"Yes, they *say*," answered Nikabrik, "but you'll notice that we hear precious little about anything he did afterwards. He just fades out of the story. How do you explain that, if he really came to life? Isn't it much more likely that he didn't, and that the stories say nothing more about him because there was nothing more to say?"

"He established the Kings and Queens," said Caspian.

"A King who has just won a great battle can usually establish himself without the help of a performing lion," said Nikabrik. There was a fierce growl, probably from Trufflehunter.

"And anyway," Nikabrik continued, "what came of the Kings and their reign? They faded too. But it's very different with the Witch. They say she ruled for a hundred years: a hundred years of winter. There's power, if you like. There's something practical."

"But, heaven and earth!" said the King, "haven't we always been told that she was the worst enemy of all? Wasn't she a tyrant ten times worse than Miraz?"

"Perhaps," said Nikabrik in a cold voice. "Perhaps she *was* for you humans, if there were any of you in those days. Perhaps she was for some of the beasts. She stamped out the Beavers, I dare say; at least there are none of them in Narnia now. But she got on all right with us Dwarfs. I'm a Dwarf and I stand by my own people. *We're* not afraid of the Witch."

"But you've joined with us," said Trufflehunter.

"Yes, and a lot of good it has done my people, so far," snapped Nikabrik. "Who is sent on all the dangerous raids? The Dwarfs. Who goes short when the rations fail? The Dwarfs. Who –?"

"Lies! All lies!" said the Badger.

"And so," said Nikabrik, whose voice now rose to a scream, "if you can't help my people, I'll go to someone who can."

"Is this open treason, Dwarf?" asked the King.

"Put that sword back in its sheath, Caspian," said Nikabrik. "Murder at council, eh? Is that your game? Don't be fool enough to try it. Do you think I'm afraid of you? There's three on my side, and three on yours."

"Come on, then," snarled Trufflehunter, but he was immediately interrupted.

"Stop, stop, stop," said Doctor Cornelius. "You go on too fast. The Witch is dead. All the stories agree on that. What does Nikabrik mean by calling on the Witch?"

That grey and terrible voice which had spoken only once before said, "Oh, *is* she?"

And then the shrill, whining voice began, "Oh, bless his heart, his dear little Majesty needn't mind about the White Lady – that's what *we* call her – being dead. The Worshipful Master Doctor is only making game of a poor old woman like me when he says that. Sweet Master Doctor, learned Master Doctor, who ever heard of a witch that really died? You can always get them back."

"Call her up," said the grey voice. "We are all ready. Draw the circle. Prepare the blue fire."

Above the steadily increasing growl of the Badger and

Cornelius's sharp "What?" rose the voice of King Caspian like thunder.

"So that is your plan, Nikabrik! Black sorcery and the calling up of an accursed ghost. And I see who your companions are – a Hag and a Wer-Wolf!"

The next minute or so was very confused. There was an animal roaring, a clash of steel; the boys and Trumpkin rushed in; Peter had a glimpse of a horrible, grey, gaunt creature, half man and half wolf, in the very act of leaping

upon a boy about his own age, and Edmund saw a badger and a Dwarf rolling on the floor in a sort of cat fight. Trumpkin found himself face to face with the Hag. Her nose and chin stuck out like a pair of nut-crackers, her dirty grey hair was flying about her face and she had just got Doctor Cornelius by the throat. At one slash of Trumpkin's sword her head rolled on the floor. Then the light was knocked over and it was all swords, teeth, claws, fists, and boots for about sixty seconds. Then silence.

"Are you all right, Ed?"

"I – I think so," panted Edmund. "I've got that brute Nikabrik, but he's still alive."

"Weights and water-bottles!" came an angry voice. "It's *me* you're sitting on. Get off. You're like a young elephant."

"Sorry, D.L.F.," said Edmund. "Is that better?"

"Ow! No!" bellowed Trumpkin. "You're putting your boot in my mouth. Go away."

"Is King Caspian anywhere?" asked Peter.

"I'm here," said a rather faint voice. "Something bit me."

They all heard the noise of someone striking a match. It was Edmund. The little flame showed his face, looking pale and dirty. He blundered about for a little, found the candle (they were no longer using the lamp, for they had run out of oil), set it on the table, and lit it. When the flame rose clear, several people scrambled to their feet. Six faces blinked at one another in the candlelight.

"We don't seem to have any enemies left," said Peter. "There's the Hag, dead." (He turned his eyes quickly away from her.) "And Nikabrik, dead too. And I suppose this thing is a Wer-Wolf. It's so long since I've seen one. Wolf's head and man's body. That means he was just turning from man into wolf at the moment he was killed. And you, I suppose, are King Caspian?"

"Yes," said the other boy. "But I've no idea who you are."

"It's the High King, King Peter," said Trumpkin.

"Your Majesty is very welcome," said Caspian.

"And so is *your* Majesty," said Peter. "I haven't come to take your place, you know, but to put you into it."

"Your Majesty," said another voice at Peter's elbow. He turned and found himself face to face with the Badger.

Peter leaned forward, put his arms round the beast and kissed the furry head: it wasn't a girlish thing for him to do, because he was the High King.

"Best of badgers," he said. "You never doubted us all through."

"No credit to me, your Majesty," said Trufflehunter. "I'm a beast and we don't change. I'm a badger, what's more, and we hold on."

"I am sorry for Nikabrik," said Caspian, "though he hated me from the first moment he saw me. He had gone sour inside from long suffering and hating. If we had won quickly he might have become a good Dwarf in the days of peace. I don't know which of us killed him. I'm glad of that."

"You're bleeding," said Peter.

"Yes, I'm bitten," said Caspian. "It was that – that wolf thing." Cleaning and bandaging the wound took a long time, and when it was done Trumpkin said, "Now. Before everything else we want some breakfast."

"But not here," said Peter.

"No," said Caspian with a shudder. "And we must send someone to take away the bodies."

"Let the vermin be flung into a pit," said Peter. "But the Dwarf we will give to his people to be buried in their own fashion."

They breakfasted at last in another of the dark cellars of Aslan's How. It was not such a breakfast as they would have chosen, for Caspian and Cornelius were thinking of venison pasties, and Peter and Edmund of buttered eggs and hot coffee, but what everyone got was a little bit of cold bear-meat (out of the boys' pockets), a lump of hard cheese, an onion, and a mug of water. But, from the way they fell to, anyone would have supposed it was delicious.

CHAPTER THIRTEEN

THE HIGH KING IN COMMAND

"Now," said Peter, as they finished their meal, "Aslan and the girls (that's Queen Susan and Queen Lucy, Caspian) are somewhere close. We don't know when he will act. In his time, no doubt, not ours. In the meantime he would like us to do what we can on our own. You say, Caspian, we are not strong enough to meet Miraz in pitched battle."

"I'm afraid not, High King," said Caspian. He was liking Peter very much, but was rather tongue-tied. It was much stranger for him to meet the great Kings out of the old stories than it was for them to meet him.

"Very well, then," said Peter, "I'll send him a challenge to single combat." No one had thought of this before.

"Please," said Caspian, "could it not be me? I want to avenge my father."

"You're wounded," said Peter. "And anyway, wouldn't he just laugh at a challenge from you? I mean, we have seen that you are a king and a warrior but he thinks of you as a kid."

"But, Sire," said the Badger, who sat very close to Peter and never took his eyes off him. "Will he accept a challenge even from you? He knows he has the stronger army."

"Very likely he won't," said Peter, "but there's always the chance. And even if he doesn't, we shall spend the best part of the day sending heralds to and fro and all that. By then Aslan may have done something. And at least I can inspect the army and strengthen the position. I will send the challenge. In fact I will write it at once. Have you pen and ink, Master Doctor?"

"A scholar is never without them, your Majesty," answered Doctor Cornelius.

"Very well, I will dictate," said Peter. And while the Doctor spread out a parchment and opened his ink-horn and sharpened his pen, Peter leant back with half-closed eyes and recalled to his mind the language in which he had written such things long ago in Narnia's golden age.

"Right," he said at last. "And now, if you are ready, Doctor?"

Doctor Cornelius dipped his pen and waited. Peter dictated as follows:

"*Peter, by the gift of Aslan, by election, by prescription, and by conquest, High King over all Kings in Narnia, Emperor of the Lone Islands and Lord of Cair Paravel, Knight of the Most Noble Order of the Lion, to Miraz, Son of Caspian the Eighth, sometime Lord Protector of Narnia and now styling himself King of Narnia, Greeting.* Have you got that?"

"*Narnia, comma, greeting,*" muttered the Doctor. "Yes, Sire."

"Then begin a new paragraph," said Peter. "*For to prevent the effusion of blood, and for the avoiding all other inconveniences likely to grow from the wars now levied in our realm of Narnia, it is our pleasure to adventure our royal person on behalf of our trusty and well-beloved Caspian in clean wager of battle to prove upon your Lordship's body that the said Caspian is lawful King under us in Narnia both by our gift and by the laws of the Telmarines, and your Lordship twice guilty of treachery both in withholding the dominion of Narnia from the said*

Caspian and in the most abhominable, – don't forget to spell it with an H, Doctor – *bloody, and unnatural murder of your kindly lord and brother King Caspian Ninth of that name. Wherefore we most heartily provoke, challenge, and defy your Lordship to the said combat and monomachy, and have sent these letters by the hand of our well beloved and royal brother Edmund, sometime King under us in Narnia, Duke of Lantern Waste and Count of the Western March, Knight of the Noble Order of the Table, to whom we have given full power of determining with your Lordship all the conditions of the said battle. Given at our lodging in Aslan's How this XII day of the month Greenroof in the first year of Caspian Tenth of Narnia.*

"That ought to do," said Peter, drawing a deep breath. "And now we must send two others with King Edmund. I think the Giant ought to be one."

"He's – he's not very clever, you know," said Caspian.

"Of course not," said Peter. "But any giant looks impressive if only he will keep quiet. And it will cheer him up. But who for the other?"

"Upon my word," said Trumpkin, "if you want someone who can kill with looks, Reepicheep would be the best."

"He would indeed, from all I hear," said Peter with a laugh. "If only he wasn't so small. They wouldn't even see him till he was close!"

"Send Glenstorm, Sire," said Trufflehunter. "No one ever laughed at a Centaur."

An hour later two great lords in the army of Miraz, the Lord Glozelle and the Lord Sopespian, strolling along their lines and picking their teeth after breakfast, looked up and saw coming down to them from the wood the Centaur and Giant Wimbleweather, whom they had seen before in battle, and between them a figure they could not recognize. Nor indeed would the other boys at Edmund's school have recognized him if they could have seen him at that moment. For Aslan had breathed on him at their meeting and a kind of greatness hung about him.

"What's to do?" said the Lord Glozelle. "An attack?"

"A parley, rather," said Sopespian. "See, they carry green branches. They are coming to surrender most likely."

"He that is walking between the Centaur and the Giant has no look of surrender in his face," said Glozelle. "Who can he be? It is not the boy Caspian."

"No indeed," said Sopespian. "This is a fell warrior, I warrant you, wherever the rebels have got him from. He is (in your Lordship's private ear) a kinglier man than ever Miraz was. And what mail he wears! None of our smiths can make the like."

"I'll wager my dappled Pomely he brings a challenge, not a surrender," said Glozelle.

"How then?" said Sopespian. "We hold the enemy in our fist here. Miraz would never be so hair-brained as to throw away his advantage on a combat."

"He might be brought to it," said Glozelle in a much lower voice.

"Softly," said Sopespian. "Step a little aside here out of earshot of those sentries. Now. Have I taken your Lordship's meaning aright?"

"If the King undertook wager of battle," whispered Glozelle, "why, either he would kill or be killed."

"So," said Sopespian, nodding his head.

"And if he killed we should have won this war."

"Certainly. And if not?"

"Why, if not, we should be as able to win it without the King's grace as with him. For I need not tell your Lordship that Miraz is no very great captain. And after that, we should be both victorious and kingless."

"And it is your meaning, my Lord, that you and I could hold this land quite as conveniently without a King as with one?"

Glozelle's face grew ugly. "Not forgetting," said he, "that it was we who first put him on the throne. And in all the years that he has enjoyed it, what fruits have come our way? What gratitude has he shown us?"

"Say no more," answered Sopespian. "But look – here comes one to fetch us to the King's tent."

When they reached Miraz's tent they saw Edmund and his two companions seated outside it and being entertained with cakes and wine, having already delivered the challenge, and withdrawn while the King was considering it. When they saw them thus at close quarters the two Telmarine lords thought all three of them very alarming.

Inside, they found Miraz, unarmed and finishing his breakfast. His face was flushed and there was a scowl on his brow.

"There!" he growled, flinging the parchment across the table to them. "See what a pack of nursery tales our jackanapes of a nephew has sent us."

"By your leave, Sire," said Glozelle. "If the young warrior whom we have just seen outside is the King Edmund mentioned in the writing, then I would not call him a nursery tale but a very dangerous knight."

"King Edmund, pah!" said Miraz. "Does your Lordship believe those old wives' fables about Peter and Edmund and the rest?"

"I believe my eyes, your Majesty," said Glozelle.

"Well, this is to no purpose," said Miraz, "but as touching the challenge, I suppose there is only one opinion between us?"

"I suppose so, indeed, Sire," said Glozelle.

"And what is that?" asked the King.

"Most infallibly to refuse it," said Glozelle. "For though I have never been called a coward, I must plainly say that to meet that young man in battle is more than my heart would serve me for. And if (as is likely) his brother, the High King, is more dangerous than he – why, on your life, my Lord King, have nothing to do with him."

"Plague on you!" cried Miraz. "It was not that sort of council I wanted. Do you think I am asking you if I should be afraid to meet this Peter (if there is such a man)? Do you think I fear him? I wanted your counsel on the policy of the matter; whether we, having the advantage, should hazard it on a wager of battle."

"To which I can only answer, your Majesty," said Glozelle, "that for all reasons the challenge should be refused. There is death in the strange knight's face."

"There you are again!" said Miraz, now thoroughly angry. "Are you trying to make it appear that I am as great a coward as your Lordship?"

"Your Majesty may say your pleasure," said Glozelle sulkily.

"You talk like an old woman, Glozelle," said the King. "What say you, my Lord Sopespian?"

"Do not touch it, Sire," was the reply. "And what your Majesty says of the policy of the thing comes in very happily. It gives your Majesty excellent grounds for a refusal without any cause for questioning your Majesty's honour or courage."

"Great Heaven!" exclaimed Miraz, jumping to his feet. "Are *you* also bewitched today? Do you think I am *looking* for grounds to refuse it? You might as well call me coward to my face."

The conversation was going exactly as the two lords wished, so they said nothing.

"I see what it is," said Miraz, after staring at them as if his eyes would start out of his head, "you are as lily-livered as hares yourselves and have the effrontery to imagine my heart after the likeness of yours! Grounds for a refusal, indeed! Excuses for not fighting! Are you soldiers? Are you Telmarines? Are you men? And if I do refuse it (as all good reasons of captaincy and martial policy urge me to do) you will think, and teach others to think, I was afraid. Is it not so?"

"No man of your Majesty's age," said Glozelle, "would be called coward by any wise soldier for refusing the combat with a great warrior in the flower of his youth."

"So I'm to be a dotard with one foot in the grave, as well as a dastard," roared Miraz. "I'll tell you what it is, my Lords. With your womanish counsels (ever shying from the true point, which is one of policy) you have done the very opposite of your intent. I had meant to refuse it. But I'll accept it. Do you hear, accept it! I'll not be shamed because some witchcraft or treason has frozen both your bloods."

"We beseech your Majesty –" said Glozelle, but Miraz had flung out of the tent and they could hear him bawling out his acceptance to Edmund.

The two lords looked at one another and chuckled quietly.

"I knew he'd do it if he were properly chafed," said Glozelle. "But I'll not forget he called me coward. It shall be paid for."

There was a great stirring at Aslan's How when the news came back and was communicated to the various creatures. Edmund, with one of Miraz's captains, had already marked out the place for the combat, and ropes and stakes had been put round it. Two Telmarines were to stand at two of the corners, and one in the middle of one side, as marshals of the lists. Three marshals for the other two corners and the other side were to be furnished by the High King. Peter was just explaining to Caspian that he could not be one, because his right to the throne was what they were fighting about, when suddenly a thick, sleepy voice said, "Your Majesty, please." Peter turned and there stood the eldest of the Bulgy Bears.

"If you please, your Majesty," he said, "I'm a bear, I am."

"To be sure, so you are, and a good bear too, I don't doubt," said Peter.

"Yes," said the Bear. "But it was always a right of the bears to supply one marshal of the lists."

"Don't let him," whispered Trumpkin to Peter. "He's a good creature, but he'll shame us all. He'll go to sleep and he *will* suck his paws. In front of the enemy too."

"I can't help that," said Peter. "Because he's quite right. The Bears had that privilege. I can't imagine how it has been remembered all these years, when so many other things have been forgotten."

"Please, your Majesty," said the Bear.

"It is your right," said Peter. "And you shall be one of the marshals. But you *must* remember not to suck your paws."

"Of course not," said the Bear in a very shocked voice.

"Why, you're doing it this minute!" bellowed Trumpkin.

The Bear whipped his paw out of his mouth and pretended he hadn't heard.

"Sire!" came a shrill voice from near the ground.

"Ah – Reepicheep!" said Peter after looking up and down and round as people usually did when addressed by the Mouse.

"Sire," said Reepicheep. "My life is ever at your command, but my honour is my own. Sire, I have among my people the only trumpeter in your Majesty's army. I had thought, perhaps, we might have been sent with the challenge. Sire, my people are grieved. Perhaps if it were your pleasure that I should be a marshal of the lists, it would content them."

A noise not unlike thunder broke out from somewhere overhead at this point, as Giant Wimbleweather burst into one of those not very intelligent laughs to which the nicer sorts of Giant are so liable. He checked himself at once and looked as grave as a turnip by the time Reepicheep discovered where the noise came from.

"I am afraid it would not do," said Peter very gravely. "Some humans are afraid of mice –"

"I had observed it, Sire," said Reepicheep.

"And it would not be quite fair to Miraz," Peter continued, "to have in sight anything that might abate the edge of his courage."

"Your Majesty is the mirror of honour," said the Mouse with one of his admirable bows. "And on this matter we have but a single mind. . . . I thought I heard someone laughing just now. If anyone present wishes to make me the subject of his wit, I am very much at his service – with my sword – whenever he has leisure."

An awful silence followed this remark, which was

broken by Peter saying, "Giant Wimbleweather and the Bear and the Centaur Glenstorm shall be our marshals. The combat will be at two hours after noon. Dinner at noon precisely."

"I say," said Edmund as they walked away, "I suppose it *is* all right. I mean, I suppose you can beat him?"

"That's what I'm fighting him to find out," said Peter.

CHAPTER FOURTEEN

HOW ALL WERE VERY BUSY

A LITTLE before two o'clock Trumpkin and the Badger sat with the rest of the creatures at the wood's edge looking across at the gleaming line of Miraz's army which was about two arrow-shots away. In between, a square space of level grass had been staked for the combat. At the two far corners stood Glozelle and Sopespian with drawn swords. At the near corners were Giant Wimbleweather and the Bulgy Bear, who in spite of all their warnings was sucking his paws and looking, to tell the truth, uncommonly silly. To make up for this, Glenstorm on the right of the lists, stock-still except when he stamped a hind hoof occasionally on the turf, looked much more imposing than the Telmarine baron who faced him on the left. Peter had just shaken hands with Edmund and the Doctor, and was now walking down to the combat. It was like the moment before the pistol goes at an important race, but very much worse.

"I wish Aslan had turned up before it came to this," said Trumpkin.

"So do I," said Trufflehunter. "But look behind you."

"Crows and crockery!" muttered the Dwarf as soon as he had done so. "What are they? Huge people – beautiful people – like gods and goddesses and giants. Hundreds and thousands of them, closing in behind us. What are they?"

"It's the Dryads and Hamadryads and Silvans," said Trufflehunter. "Aslan has waked them."

"Humph!" said the Dwarf. "That'll be very useful if the

enemy try any treachery. But it won't help the High King very much if Miraz proves handier with his sword."

The Badger said nothing, for now Peter and Miraz were entering the lists from opposite ends, both on foot, both in chain shirts, with helmets and shields. They advanced till they were close together. Both bowed and seemed to speak, but it was impossible to hear what they said. Next moment the two swords flashed in the sunlight. For a second the clash could be heard but it was immediately drowned because both armies began shouting like crowds at a football match.

"Well done, Peter, oh, well done!" shouted Edmund as he saw Miraz reel back a whole pace and a half. "Follow it up, quick!" And Peter did, and for a few seconds it looked as if the fight might be won. But then Miraz pulled himself together – began to make real use of his height and weight. "Miraz! Miraz! The King! The King!" came the roar of the Telmarines. Caspian and Edmund grew white with sickening anxiety.

"Peter is taking some dreadful knocks," said Edmund.

"Hullo!" said Caspian. "What's happening now?"

"Both falling apart," said Edmund. "A bit blown, I expect. Watch. Ah, now they're beginning again, more scientifically this time. Circling round and round, feeling each other's defences."

"I'm afraid this Miraz knows his work," muttered the Doctor. But hardly had he said this when there was such a clapping and baying and throwing up of hoods among the Old Narnians that it was nearly deafening.

"What was it? What was it?" asked the Doctor. "My old eyes missed it."

"The High King has pricked him in the arm-pit," said

Caspian, still clapping. "Just where the arm-hole of the hauberk let the point through. First blood."

"It's looking ugly again now, though," said Edmund. "Peter's not using his shield properly. He must be hurt in the left arm."

It was only too true. Everyone could see that Peter's shield hung limp. The shouting of the Telmarines redoubled.

"You've seen more battles than I," said Caspian. "Is there any chance now?"

"Precious little," said Edmund. "I suppose he might *just* do it. With luck."

"Oh, why did we let it happen at all?" said Caspian.

Suddenly all the shouting on both sides died down. Edmund was puzzled for a moment. Then he said, "Oh, I see. They've both agreed to a rest. Come on, Doctor. You and I may be able to do something for the High King." They ran down to the lists and Peter came outside the ropes to meet them, his face red and sweaty, his chest heaving.

"Is your left arm wounded?" asked Edmund.

"It's not exactly a wound," Peter said. "I got the full weight of his shoulder on my shield – like a load of bricks – and the rim of the shield drove into my wrist. I don't think it's broken, but it might be a sprain. If you could tie it up very tight I think I could manage."

While they were doing this, Edmund asked anxiously, "What do you think of him, Peter?"

"Tough," said Peter. "Very tough. I have a chance if I can keep him on the hop till his weight and short wind come against him – in this hot sun too. To tell the truth, I haven't much chance else. Give my love to – to everyone at home, Ed, if he gets me. Here he comes into the lists again.

So long, old chap. Good-bye, Doctor. And I say, Ed, say something specially nice to Trumpkin. He's been a brick."

Edmund couldn't speak. He walked back with the Doctor to his own lines with a sick feeling in his stomach.

But the new bout went well. Peter now seemed to be able to make some use of his shield, and he certainly made good use of his feet. He was almost playing Tig with Miraz now, keeping out of range, shifting his ground, making the enemy work.

"Coward!" booed the Telmarines. "Why don't you stand up to him? Don't you like it, eh? Thought you'd come to fight, not dance. Yah!"

"Oh, I do hope he won't listen to them," said Caspian.

"Not he," said Edmund. "You don't know him – Oh!" – for Miraz had got in a blow at last, on Peter's helmet. Peter staggered, slipped sideways, and fell on one knee. The roar of the Telmarines rose like the noise of the sea. "Now, Miraz," they yelled. "Now. Quick! Quick! Kill him." But indeed there was no need to egg the usurper on. He was on top of Peter already. Edmund bit his lips till the blood came, as the sword flashed down on Peter. It looked as if it would slash off his head. Thank heavens! it had glanced down his right shoulder. The Dwarf-wrought mail was sound and did not break.

"Great Scott!" cried Edmund. "He's up again. Peter, go it, Peter."

"I couldn't see what happened," said the Doctor. "How did he do it?"

"Grabbed Miraz's arm as it came down," said Trumpkin, dancing with delight. "There's a man for you! Uses his enemy's arm as a ladder. The High King! The High King! Up, Old Narnia!"

"Look," said Trufflehunter. "Miraz is angry. It is good."

They were certainly at it hammer and tongs now: such a flurry of blows that it seemed impossible for either not to be killed. As the excitement grew, the shouting almost died away. The spectators were holding their breath. It was most horrible and most magnificent.

A great shout arose from the Old Narnians. Miraz was down – not struck by Peter, but face downwards, having tripped on a tussock. Peter stepped back, waiting for him to rise.

"Oh bother, bother, bother," said Edmund to himself. "Need he be as gentlemanly as all that? I suppose he must. Comes of being a Knight *and* a High King. I suppose it is what Aslan would like. But that brute will be up again in a minute and then –"

But "that brute" never rose. The Lords Glozelle and Sopespian had their own plans ready. As soon as they saw their King down they leaped into the lists crying, "Treachery! Treachery! The Narnian traitor has stabbed him in the back while he lay helpless. To arms! To arms, Telmar!"

Peter hardly understood what was happening. He saw two big men running towards him with drawn swords. Then the third Telmarine had leaped over the ropes on his left. "To arms, Narnia! Treachery!" Peter shouted. If all three had set upon him at once he would never have spoken again. But Glozelle stopped to stab his own King dead where he lay: "That's for your insult, this morning," he whispered as the blade went home. Peter swung to face Sopespian, slashed his legs from under him and, with the back-cut of the same stroke, walloped off his head. Edmund was now at his side crying, "Narnia, Narnia! The Lion!" The whole Telmarine army was rushing towards them. But now the Giant was stamping forward, stooping low and swinging his club. The Centaurs charged. *Twang, twang* behind and *hiss, hiss* overhead came the archery of Dwarfs. Trumpkin was fighting at his left. Full battle was joined.

"Come back, Reepicheep, you little ass!" shouted Peter. "You'll only be killed. This is no place for mice." But the ridiculous little creatures were dancing in and out among the feet of both armies, jabbing with their swords. Many a Telmarine warrior that day felt his foot suddenly pierced as if by a dozen skewers, hopped on one leg cursing the pain, and fell as often as not. If he fell, the mice finished him off; if he did not, someone else did.

But almost before the Old Narnians were really warmed to their work they found the enemy giving way. Tough-looking warriors turned white, gazed in terror not on the Old Narnians but on something behind them, and then flung down their weapons, shrieking, "The Wood! The Wood! The end of the world!"

But soon neither their cries nor the sound of weapons could be heard any more, for both were drowned in the ocean-like roar of the Awakened Trees as they plunged through the ranks of Peter's army, and then on, in pursuit of the Telmarines. Have you ever stood at the edge of a great wood on a high ridge when a wild south-wester broke over it in full fury on an autumn evening? Imagine that sound. And then imagine that the wood, instead of being fixed to one place, was rushing *at* you; and was no longer trees but huge people; yet still like trees because their long arms waved like branches and their heads tossed and leaves fell round them in showers. It was like that for the Telmarines. It was a little alarming even for the

Narnians. In a few minutes all Miraz's followers were running down to the Great River in the hope of crossing the bridge to the town of Beruna and there defending themselves behind ramparts and closed gates.

They reached the river, but there was no bridge. It had disappeared since yesterday. Then utter panic and horror fell upon them and they all surrendered.

But what had happened to the bridge?

Early that morning, after a few hours' sleep, the girls had

waked, to see Aslan standing over them and to hear his voice saying, "We will make holiday." They rubbed their eyes and looked round them. The trees had all gone but could still be seen moving away towards Aslan's How in a dark mass. Bacchus and the Maenads – his fierce, madcap girls – and Silenus were still with them. Lucy, fully rested, jumped up. Everyone was awake, everyone was laughing, flutes were playing, cymbals clashing. Animals, not Talking Animals, were crowding in upon them from every direction.

"What is it, Aslan?" said Lucy, her eyes dancing and her feet wanting to dance.

"Come, children," said he. "Ride on my back again today."

"Oh, lovely!" cried Lucy, and both girls climbed on to the warm golden back as they had done no one knew how many years before. Then the whole party moved off – Aslan leading, Bacchus and his Maenads leaping, rushing, and turning somersaults, the beasts frisking round them, and Silenus and his donkey bringing up the rear.

They turned a little to the right, raced down a steep hill, and found the long Bridge of Beruna in front of them. Before they had begun to cross it, however, up out of the water came a great wet, bearded head, larger than a man's, crowned with rushes. It looked at Aslan and out of its mouth a deep voice came.

"Hail, Lord," it said. "Loose my chains."

"Who on earth is *that*?" whispered Susan.

"I think it's the river-god, but hush," said Lucy.

"Bacchus," said Aslan. "Deliver him from his chains."

"That means the bridge, I expect," thought Lucy. And so it did. Bacchus and his people splashed forward into the shallow water, and a minute later the most curious things began happening. Great, strong trunks of ivy came curling up all the piers of the bridge, growing as quickly as a fire grows, wrapping the stones round, splitting, breaking, separating them. The walls of the bridge turned into hedges gay with hawthorn for a moment and then disappeared as the whole thing with a rush and a rumble collapsed into the swirling water. With much splashing, screaming, and laughter the revellers waded or swam or danced across the ford ("Hurrah! It's the Ford of Beruna again now!" cried the girls) and up the bank on the far side and into the town.

Everyone in the streets fled before their faces. The first house they came to was a school: a girls' school, where a lot of Narnian girls, with their hair done very tight and ugly tight collars round their necks and thick tickly stockings on their legs, were having a history lesson. The sort of "History" that was taught in Narnia under Miraz's rule was duller than the truest history you ever read and less true than the most exciting adventure story.

"If you don't attend, Gwendolen," said the mistress, "and stop looking out of the window, I shall have to give you an order-mark."

"But please, Miss Prizzle –" began Gwendolen.

"Did you hear what I said, Gwendolen?" asked Miss Prizzle.

"But please, Miss Prizzle," said Gwendolen, "there's a LION!"

"Take two order-marks for talking nonsense," said Miss Prizzle. "And now –" A roar interrupted her. Ivy came curling in at the windows of the classroom. The walls became a mass of shimmering green, and leafy branches arched overhead where the ceiling had been. Miss Prizzle found she was standing on grass in a forest glade. She clutched at her desk to steady herself, and found that the desk was a rose-bush. Wild people such as she had never even imagined were crowding round her. Then she saw the Lion, screamed and fled, and with her fled her class, who were mostly dumpy, prim little girls with fat legs. Gwendolen hesitated.

"You'll stay with us, sweetheart?" said Aslan.

"Oh, *may* I? Thank you, thank you," said Gwendolen. Instantly she joined hands with two of the Maenads, who whirled her round in a merry dance and helped her take off some of the unnecessary and uncomfortable clothes that she was wearing.

Wherever they went in the little town of Beruna it was the same. Most of the people fled, a few joined them. When they left the town they were a larger and a merrier company.

They swept on across the level fields on the north bank, or left bank, of the river. At every farm animals came out to join them. Sad old donkeys who had never known joy grew suddenly young again; chained dogs broke their chains; horses kicked their carts to pieces and came trotting along with them – clop-clop – kicking up the mud and whinnying.

At a well in a yard they met a man who was beating a boy. The stick burst into flower in the man's hand. He tried to drop it, but it stuck to his hand. His arm became a branch, his body the trunk of a tree, his feet took root. The boy, who had been crying a moment before, burst out laughing and joined them.

At a little town half-way to Beaversdam, where two rivers met, they came to another school, where a tired-looking girl was teaching arithmetic to a number of boys who looked very like pigs. She looked out of the window and saw the divine revellers singing up the street and a stab of joy went through her heart. Aslan stopped right under the window and looked up at her.

"Oh, don't, don't," she said. "I'd love to. But I mustn't. I

must stick to my work. And the children would be frightened if they saw you."

"Frightened?" said the most pig-like of the boys. "Who's she talking to out of the window? Let's tell the inspector she talks to people out of the window when she ought to be teaching us."

"Let's go and see who it is," said another boy, and they all came crowding to the window. But as soon as their mean little faces looked out, Bacchus gave a great cry of *Euan, euoi-oi-oi-oi* and the boys all began howling with fright and trampling one another down to get out of the door and jumping out of the windows. And it was said afterwards (whether truly or not) that those particular little boys were never seen again, but that there were a lot of very fine little pigs in that part of the country which had never been there before.

"Now, Dear Heart," said Aslan to the Mistress: and she jumped down and joined them.

At Beaversdam they re-crossed the river and came east again along the southern bank. They came to a little cottage where a child stood in the doorway crying. "Why are you crying, my love?" asked Aslan. The child, who had never seen a picture of a lion, was not afraid of him. "Auntie's very ill," she said. "She's going to die." Then Aslan went to go in at the door of the cottage, but it was too small for him. So, when he had got his head through, he pushed with his shoulders (Lucy and Susan fell off when he did this) and lifted the whole house up and it fell backwards and apart. And there, still in her bed, though the bed was now in the open air, lay a little old woman who looked as if she had Dwarf blood in her. She was at death's door, but when she opened her eyes and saw the bright, hairy head of the lion staring into her face, she did not scream or faint. She said, "Oh, Aslan! I knew it was true. I've been waiting for this all my life. Have you come to take me away?"

"Yes, Dearest," said Aslan. "But not the long journey yet." And as he spoke, like the flush creeping along the underside of a cloud at sunrise, the colour came back to her white face and her eyes grew bright and she sat up and said, "Why, I do declare I feel *that* better. I think I could take a little breakfast this morning."

"Here you are, mother," said Bacchus, dipping a pitcher in the cottage well and handing it to her. But what was in it now was not water but the richest wine, red as red-currant jelly, smooth as oil, strong as beef, warming as tea, cool as dew.

"Eh, you've done something to our well," said the old woman. "That makes a nice change, that does." And she jumped out of bed.

"Ride on me," said Aslan, and added to Susan and Lucy, "You two queens will have to run now."

"But we'd like that just as well," said Susan. And off they went again.

And so at last, with leaping and dancing and singing, with music and laughter and roaring and barking and neighing, they all came to the place where Miraz's army stood flinging down their swords and holding up their hands, and Peter's army, still holding their weapons and breathing hard, stood round them with stern and glad faces. And the first thing that happened was that the old woman slipped off Aslan's back and ran across to Caspian and they embraced one another; for she was his old nurse.

CHAPTER FIFTEEN

ASLAN MAKES A DOOR IN THE AIR

At the sight of Aslan the cheeks of the Telmarine soldiers became the colour of cold gravy, their knees knocked together, and many fell on their faces. They had not believed in lions and this made their fear greater. Even the Red Dwarfs, who knew that he came as a friend, stood with open mouths and could not speak. Some of the Black Dwarfs, who had been of Nikabrik's party, began to edge away. But all the Talking Beasts surged round the Lion, with purrs and grunts and squeaks and whinneys of delight, fawning on him with their tails, rubbing against him, touching him reverently with their noses and going to and fro under his body and between his legs. If you have ever seen a little cat loving a big dog whom it knows and trusts, you will have a pretty good picture of their behaviour. Then Peter, leading Caspian, forced his way through the crowd of animals.

"This is Caspian, Sir," he said. And Caspian knelt and kissed the Lion's paw.

"Welcome, Prince," said Aslan. "Do you feel yourself sufficient to take up the Kingship of Narnia?"

"I – I don't think I do, Sir," said Caspian. "I'm only a kid."

"Good," said Aslan. "If you had felt yourself sufficient, it would have been a proof that you were not. Therefore, under us and under the High King, you shall be King of Narnia, Lord of Cair Paravel, and Emperor of the Lone Islands. You and your heirs while your race lasts. And your coronation – but what have we here?" For at that moment a curious little procession was approaching – eleven Mice, six of whom carried between them something on a litter made of branches, but the litter was no bigger than a large atlas. No one has ever seen mice more woebegone than these. They were plastered with mud – some with blood too – and their ears were down and their whiskers drooped and their tails dragged in the grass, and their leader piped on his slender pipe a melancholy tune. On the litter lay what seemed little better than a damp heap of fur; all that was left of Reepicheep. He was still breathing, but more dead than alive, gashed with innumerable wounds, one paw crushed, and, where his tail had been, a bandaged stump.

"Now, Lucy," said Aslan.

Lucy had her diamond bottle out in a moment. Though only a drop was needed on each of Reepicheep's wounds, the wounds were so many that there was a long and anxious silence before she had finished and the Master Mouse sprang from the litter. His hand went at once to his sword hilt, with the other he twirled his whiskers. He bowed.

"Hail, Aslan!" came his shrill voice. "I have the honour –" But then he suddenly stopped.

The fact was that he still had no tail – whether that Lucy had forgotten it or that her cordial, though it could heal wounds, could not make things grow again. Reepicheep became aware of his loss as he made his bow; perhaps it altered something in his balance. He looked over his right shoulder. Failing to see his tail, he strained his neck further till he had to turn his shoulders and his whole body followed. But by that time his hind-quarters had turned too and were out of sight. Then he strained his neck looking over his shoulder again, with the same result. Only after he had turned completely round three times did he realize the dreadful truth.

"I am confounded," said Reepicheep to Aslan. "I am completely out of countenance. I must crave your indulgence for appearing in this unseemly fashion."

"It becomes you very well, Small One," said Aslan.

"All the same," replied Reepicheep, "if anything could

be done . . . Perhaps her Majesty?" and here he bowed to Lucy.

"But what do you want with a tail?" asked Aslan.

"Sir," said the Mouse, "I can eat and sleep and die for my King without one. But a tail is the honour and glory of a Mouse."

"I have sometimes wondered, friend," said Aslan, "whether you do not think too much about your honour."

"Highest of all High Kings," said Reepicheep, "permit me to remind you that a very small size has been bestowed on us Mice, and if we did not guard our dignity, some (who weigh worth by inches) would allow themselves very unsuitable pleasantries at our expense. That is why I have been at some pains to make it known that no one who does not wish to feel this sword as near his heart as I can reach shall talk in my presence about Traps or Toasted Cheese or Candles: no, Sir – not the tallest fool in Narnia!" Here he glared very fiercely up at Wimbleweather, but the Giant, who was always a stage behind everyone else, had not yet discovered what was being talked about down at his feet, and so missed the point.

"Why have your followers all drawn *their* swords, may I ask?" said Aslan.

"May it please your High Majesty," said the second Mouse, whose name was Peepiceek, "we are all waiting to cut off our own tails if our Chief must go without his. We will not bear the shame of wearing an honour which is denied to the High Mouse."

"Ah!" roared Aslan. "You have conquered me. You have great hearts. Not for the sake of your dignity, Reepicheep, but for the love that is between you and your people, and still more for the kindness your people showed me long ago when you ate away the cords that bound me on the Stone Table (and it was then, though you have long forgotten it, that you began to be *Talking* Mice), you shall have your tail again."

Before Aslan had finished speaking the new tail was in its place. Then, at Aslan's command, Peter bestowed the Knighthood of the Order of the Lion on Caspian, and Caspian, as soon as he was knighted, himself bestowed it on Trufflehunter and Trumpkin and Reepicheep, and made Doctor Cornelius his Lord Chancellor, and confirmed the Bulgy Bear in his hereditary office of Marshal of the Lists. And there was great applause.

After this the Telmarine soldiers, firmly but without taunts or blows, were taken across the ford and all put under lock and key in the town of Beruna and given beef and beer. They made a great fuss about wading in the river, for they all hated and feared running water just as much as they hated and feared woods and animals. But in the end the nuisance was over: and then the nicest parts of that long day began.

Lucy, sitting close to Aslan and divinely comfortable, wondered what the trees were doing. At first she thought they were merely dancing; they were certainly going round slowly in two circles, one from left to right and the other from right to left. Then she noticed that they kept throwing something down in the centre of both circles. Sometimes she thought they were cutting off long strands of their hair; at other times it looked as if they were breaking off bits of their fingers – but, if so, they had plenty of fingers to spare and it did not hurt them. But whatever they were throwing down, when it reached the ground, it became brushwood or dry sticks. Then three or four of the Red Dwarfs came forward with their tinder boxes and set light to the pile, which first crackled, and then blazed, and finally roared as a woodland bonfire on midsummer night ought to do. And everyone sat down in a wide circle round it.

Then Bacchus and Silenus and the Maenads began a dance, far wilder than the dance of the trees; not merely a dance for fun and beauty (though it was that too) but a magic dance of plenty, and where their hands touched, and where their feet fell, the feast came into existence – sides of roasted meat that filled the grove with delicious smell, and wheaten cakes and oaten cakes, honey and many-coloured sugars and cream as thick as porridge and as smooth as still water, peaches, nectarines, pomegranates, pears, grapes, strawberries, raspberries – pyramids and cataracts of fruit. Then, in great wooden cups and bowls and mazers, wreathed with ivy, came the wines; dark, thick ones like syrups of mulberry juice, and clear red ones like red jellies liquefied, and yellow wines

and green wines and yellow-green and greenish-yellow.

But for the tree people different fare was provided. When Lucy saw Clodsley Shovel and his moles scuffling up the turf in various places (which Bacchus had pointed out to them) and realized that the trees were going to eat *earth* it gave her rather a shudder. But when she saw the earths that were actually brought to them she felt quite different. They began with a rich brown loam that looked almost exactly like chocolate; so like chocolate, in fact, that Edmund tried a piece of it, but he did not find it at all nice. When the rich loam had taken the edge off their hunger, the trees turned to an earth of the kind you see in Somerset, which is almost pink. They said it was lighter and sweeter. At the cheese stage they had a chalky soil, and then went on to delicate confections of the finest gravels powdered with choice silver sand. They drank very little wine, and it made the Hollies very talkative: for the most part they quenched their thirst with deep draughts of mingled dew and rain, flavoured with forest flowers and the airy taste of the thinnest clouds.

Thus Aslan feasted the Narnians till long after the

sunset had died away, and the stars had come out; and the great fire, now hotter but less noisy, shone like a beacon in the dark woods, and the frightened Telmarines saw it from far away and wondered what it might mean. The best thing of all about this feast was that there was no breaking up or going away, but as the talk grew quieter and slower, one after another would begin to nod and finally drop off to sleep with feet towards the fire and good friends on either side, till at last there was silence all round the circle, and the chattering of water over stone at the Ford of Beruna could be heard once more. But all night Aslan and the

Moon gazed upon each other with joyful and unblinking eyes.

Next day messengers (who were chiefly squirrels and birds) were sent all over the country with a proclamation to the scattered Telmarines – including, of course, the prisoners in Beruna. They were told that Caspian was now King and that Narnia would henceforth belong to the Talking Beasts and the Dwarfs and Dryads and Fauns and other creatures quite as much as to the men. Any who

chose to stay under the new conditions might do so; but for those who did not like the idea, Aslan would provide another home. Anyone who wished to go there must come to Aslan and the Kings at the Ford of Beruna by noon on the fifth day. You may imagine that this caused plenty of head-scratching among the Telmarines. Some of them, chiefly the young ones, had, like Caspian, heard stories of the Old Days and were delighted that they had come back. They were already making friends with the creatures. These all decided to stay in Narnia. But most of the older men, especially those who had been important under Miraz, were sulky and had no wish to live in a country where they could not rule the roost. "Live here with a lot of blooming performing animals! No fear," they said. "And ghosts too," some added with a shudder. "That's what those there Dryads really are. It's not canny." They were also suspicious. "I don't trust 'em," they said. "Not with that awful Lion and all. He won't keep his claws off us long, *you'll* see." But then they were equally suspicious of his offer to give them a new home. "Take us off to his den and eat us one by one most likely," they muttered. And the more they talked to one another the sulkier and more suspicious they became. But on the appointed day more than half of them turned up.

At one end of the glade Aslan had caused to be set up two stakes of wood, higher than a man's head and about three feet apart. A third, and lighter, piece of wood was bound across them at the top, uniting them, so that the whole thing looked like a doorway from nowhere into nowhere. In front of this stood Aslan himself with Peter on his right and Caspian on his left. Grouped round them were Susan and Lucy, Trumpkin and Trufflehunter, the Lord Cornelius, Glenstorm, Reepicheep, and others. The children and the Dwarfs had made good use of the royal wardrobes in what had been the castle of Miraz and was now the castle of Caspian, and what with silk and cloth of gold, with snowy linen glancing through slashed sleeves, with silver mail shirts and jewelled sword-hilts, with gilt helmets and feathered bonnets, they were almost too bright to look at. Even the beasts wore rich chains about their necks. Yet nobody's eyes were on them or the children. The living and strokable gold of Aslan's mane outshone them all. The rest of the Old Narnians stood down each side of the glade. At the far end stood the

Telmarines. The sun shone brightly and pennants fluttered in the light wind.

"Men of Telmar," said Aslan, "you who seek a new land, hear my words. I will send you all to your own country, which I know and you do not."

"We don't remember Telmar. We don't know where it is. We don't know what it is like," grumbled the Telmarines.

"You came into Narnia out of Telmar," said Aslan. "But you came into Telmar from another place. You do not belong to this world at all. You came hither, certain generations ago, out of that same world to which the High King Peter belongs."

At this, half the Telmarines began whimpering, "There you are. Told you so. He's going to kill us all, send us right out of the world," and the other half began throwing out their chests and slapping one another on the back and whispering, "There you are. Might have guessed we didn't belong to this place with all its queer, nasty, unnatural creatures. We're of royal blood, you'll see." And even Caspian and Cornelius and the children turned to Aslan with looks of amazement on their faces.

"Peace," said Aslan in the low voice which was nearest to his growl. The earth seemed to shake a little and every living thing in the grove became still as stone.

"You, Sir Caspian," said Aslan, "might have known that you could be no true King of Narnia unless, like the Kings of old, you were a son of Adam and came from the world of Adam's sons. And so you are. Many years ago in that world, in a deep sea of that world which is called the South Sea, a shipload of pirates were driven by storm on an island. And there they did as pirates would: killed the natives and took the native women for wives, and made palm wine, and drank and were drunk, and lay in the shade of the palm trees, and woke up and quarrelled, and sometimes killed one another. And in one of these frays six were put to flight by the rest and fled with their women into the centre of the island and up a mountain, and went, as they thought, into a cave to hide. But it was one of the magical places of that world, one of the chinks or chasms between that world and this. There were many chinks or chasms between worlds in old times, but they have grown rarer. This was one of the last: I do not say *the* last. And so they fell, or rose, or blundered, or dropped right through, and found themselves in this world, in the Land of Telmar which was then unpeopled. But why it was unpeopled is a long story: I will not tell it now. And in Telmar their descendants lived and became a fierce and proud people; and after many generations there was a famine in Telmar and they invaded Narnia, which was then in some disorder (but that also would be a long story), and conquered it and ruled it. Do you mark all this well, King Caspian?"

"I do indeed, Sir," said Caspian. "I was wishing that I came of a more honourable lineage."

"You come of the Lord Adam and the Lady Eve," said Aslan. "And that is both honour enough to erect the head of the poorest beggar, and shame enough to bow the shoulders of the greatest emperor on earth. Be content."

Caspian bowed.

"And now," said Aslan, "you men and women of Telmar, will you go back to that island in the world of men from which your fathers first came? It is no bad place. The race of those pirates who first found it has died out, and it is without inhabitants. There are good wells of fresh water, and fruitful soil, and timber for building, and fish in the lagoons; and the other men of that world have not yet discovered it. The chasm is open for your return; but this I must warn you, that once you have gone through, it will close behind you for ever. There will be no more commerce between the worlds by that door."

There was silence for a moment. Then a burly, decent-looking fellow among the Telmarine soldiers pushed forward and said:

"Well, I'll take the offer."

"It is well chosen," said Aslan. "And because you have spoken first, strong magic is upon you. Your future in that world shall be good. Come forth."

The man, now a little pale, came forward. Aslan and his court drew aside, leaving him free access to the empty doorway of the stakes.

"Go through it, my son," said Aslan, bending towards him and touching the man's nose with his own. As soon as the Lion's breath came about him, a new look came into the man's eyes – startled, but not unhappy – as if he were trying to remember something. Then he squared his shoulders and walked into the Door.

Everyone's eyes were fixed on him. They saw the three pieces of wood, and through them the trees and grass and sky of Narnia. They saw the man between the doorposts: then, in one second, he had vanished utterly.

From the other end of the glade the remaining Telmarines set up a wailing. "Ugh! What's happened to him? Do you mean to murder us? We won't go that way." And then one of the clever Telmarines said:

"We don't see any other world through those sticks. If

you want us to believe in it, why doesn't one of *you* go? All your own friends are keeping well away from the sticks."

Instantly Reepicheep stood forward and bowed. "If *my* example can be of any service, Aslan," he said, "I will take eleven mice through that arch at your bidding without a moment's delay."

"Nay, little one," said Aslan, laying his velvety paw ever so lightly on Reepicheep's head. "They would do dreadful things to you in that world. They would show you at fairs. It is others who must lead."

"Come on," said Peter suddenly to Edmund and Lucy. "Our time's up."

"What do you mean?" said Edmund.

"This way," said Susan, who seemed to know all about it. "Back into the trees. We've got to change."

"Change what?" asked Lucy.

"Our clothes, of course," said Susan. "Nice fools we'd look on the platform of an English station in *these*."

"But our other things are at Caspian's castle," said Edmund.

"No, they're not," said Peter, still leading the way into the thickest wood. "They're all here. They were brought down in bundles this morning. It's all arranged."

"Was that what Aslan was talking to you and Susan about this morning?" asked Lucy.

"Yes – that and other things," said Peter, his face very solemn. "I can't tell it to you all. There were things he wanted to say to Su and me because we're not coming back to Narnia."

"Never?" cried Edmund and Lucy in dismay.

"Oh, you two are," answered Peter. "At least, from what he said, I'm pretty sure he means you to get back some day. But not Su and me. He says we're getting too old."

"Oh, Peter," said Lucy. "What awful bad luck. Can you bear it?"

"Well, I think I can," said Peter. "It's all rather different from what I thought. You'll understand when it comes to your last time. But, quick, here are our things."

It was odd, and not very nice, to take off their royal clothes and to come back in their school things (not very fresh now) into that great assembly. One or two of the nastier Telmarines jeered. But the other creatures all cheered and rose up in honour of Peter the High King, and Queen Susan of the Horn, and King Edmund, and Queen Lucy. There were affectionate and (on Lucy's part) tearful farewells with all their old friends – animal kisses, and hugs from Bulgy Bears, and hands wrung by Trumpkin, and a last tickly, whiskerish embrace with Trufflehunter. And of course Caspian offered the Horn back to Susan and of course Susan told him to keep it. And then, wonderfully and terribly, it was farewell to

Aslan himself, and Peter took his place with Susan's hands on his shoulders and Edmund's on hers and Lucy's on his and the first of the Telmarine's on Lucy's, and so in a long line they moved forward to the Door. After that came a moment which is hard to describe, for the children seemed to be seeing three things at once. One was the mouth of a cave opening into the glaring green and blue of an island in the Pacific, where all the Telmarines would find themselves the moment they were through the Door. The second was a glade in Narnia, the faces of Dwarfs and Beasts, the deep eyes of Aslan, and the white patches on the Badger's cheeks. But the third (which rapidly swallowed up the other two) was the grey, gravelly surface of a platform in a country station, and a seat with luggage round it, where they were all sitting as if they had never moved from it – a little flat and dreary for a moment after all they had been through, but also, unexpectedly, nice in its own way, what with the familiar railway smell and the English sky and the summer term before them.

"Well!" said Peter. "We *have* had a time."

"Bother!" said Edmund. "I've left my new torch in Narnia."

The Chronicles of Narnia

by C. S. Lewis

C. S. Lewis's wit and wisdom, his blend of excitement and adventure with fantasy, have made this magnificent series beloved of many generations of readers. The final book, *The Last Battle*, won the Carnegie Medal for 1956.

Each of the seven titles is a complete story in itself, but all take place in the magical land of Narnia. Guided by the noble Lion Aslan, the children learn that evil and treachery can only be overcome by courage, loyalty and great sacrifice.

The titles, in suggested reading order, are as follows:

The Magician's Nephew
The Lion, the Witch and the Wardrobe
The Horse and His Boy
Prince Caspian
The Voyage of the Dawn Treader
The Silver Chair
The Last Battle

The Chronicles of Narnia

C. S. Lewis

Each of the seven titles is a complete story in itself, but all take place in the magical land of Narnia. Guided by the noble Lion Aslan, the children learn that evil and treachery can only be overcome by courage, loyalty and great sacrifice.

In reading order:

The Magician's Nephew
The Lion, The Witch and the Wardrobe
The Horse and His Boy
Prince Caspian
The Voyage of the *Dawn Treader*
The Silver Chair
The Last Battle
Narnia Gift Pack
(all seven titles in a slipcase)

The Chronicles of Narnia are also available in larger format editions.